YOU SHALL RIDE WITH ME

Mirabella turned to face him. "Do you actually think I would ride anywhere with you after your insufferable behavior last night?"

"I sought only to play your knight."

"I had no need of your assistance."

"That is not how I viewed the situation. You nearly started a riot with that low-cut clinging gown of yours. At the very least, you could have worn some lace to fill in the bodice."

"A *true gentleman* would not dare comment on my lack of lace, or—or . . ."

"How fortunate for me, then, that you deem me a rogue. Rogues, I hear, are forgiven a great many transgressions."

"You, my lord, are forgiven nothing."

"It isn't your forgiveness I seek."

Other **Regency Romances**
from Avon Books

CLARISSA *by Cathleen Clare*
FAIR SCHEMER *by Sally Martin*
LORD FORTUNE'S PRIZE *by Nancy Richards-Akers*
THE MISCHIEVOUS MAID *by Rebecca Robbins*
THE MUCH MALIGNED LORD *by Barbara Reeves*

Coming Soon

DEIRDRE AND DON JUAN *by Jo Beverley*

Avon Books are available at special quantity discounts for bulk purchases for sales promotions, premiums, fund raising or educational use. Special books, or book excerpts, can also be created to fit specific needs.

For details write or telephone the office of the Director of Special Markets, Avon Books, Dept. FP, 1350 Avenue of the Americas, New York, New York 10019, 1-800-238-0658.

The Unmatchable Miss Mirabella

GILLIAN GREY

AVON BOOKS NEW YORK

If you purchased this book without a cover, you should be aware that this book is stolen property. It was reported as "unsold and destroyed" to the publisher, and neither the author nor the publisher has received any payment for this "stripped book."

THE UNMATCHABLE MISS MIRABELLA is an original publication of Avon Books. This work has never before appeared in book form. This work is a novel. Any similarity to actual persons or events is purely coincidental.

AVON BOOKS
A division of
The Hearst Corporation
1350 Avenue of the Americas
New York, New York 10019

Copyright © 1993 by Gillian Grey
Published by arrangement with the author
Library of Congress Catalog Card Number: 93-90347
ISBN: 0-380-77399-6

All rights reserved, which includes the right to reproduce this book or portions thereof in any form whatsoever except as provided by the U.S. Copyright Law. For information address Avon Books.

First Avon Books Printing: November 1993

AVON TRADEMARK REG. U.S. PAT. OFF. AND IN OTHER COUNTRIES, MARCA REGISTRADA, HECHO EN U.S.A.

Printed in the U.S.A.

RA 10 9 8 7 6 5 4 3 2 1

In loving memory of my mother,
Betty J. Kindblom Coleman,
who shared her love, her life, and her books

1

Miss Mirabella Lavinia Darlington, late of tiger-sketching in Bengal, arrived at her godmama's recuperative country estate in the Cotswolds just as pandemonium erupted.

Mirabella no sooner alighted from her carriage than she spied a gaggle of her godmama's maids rushing about the lawns, peering under trees and hedges frantically yoo-hooing for someone by the name of Max.

Mirabella thought nothing of joining the search. She was very much accustomed to her godmama's eccentric household, filled as it was with a mishmash of lost souls mending their spirits and redirecting their lives. Her godmama, Penelope Barrington, was revered among the *ton* not only for her good name but also for her generous heart.

Stormhaven, her most prized country estate (and the outlandish Penelope owned a good many estates, due to her uncanny habit of marrying well-to-do gentlemen—both young and old—who invariably had one foot in the grave), was nestled amid the rolling lands near Stow-on-the-Wold, and had become a much-sought-after retreat. Both peers and vagabonds found solace within the sprawling place where former street urchins and pickpockets could become respectable maids or grooms, where a sickly duchess could recuperate in peace, or a tired marquis discover fresh reason for living.

In truth, Mirabella was one of those who sought peace and comfort there. She was a broken-winged bird retreating to the familiar nest she'd known during her childhood. Though she had lived in various locales around the world, Stormhaven was the only place she'd ever called home.

She'd lost her dear, beloved father, Percy, little more than a year ago. A huge portion of her heart had died along with him, for he had been provider and teacher, father and friend. Mirabella had no sooner gone into mourning than she'd noticed the buzz of activity flourishing around her as fops, dandies, and supposed gentlemen who were always in dun territory began to cast glances her way. Her father had bequeathed her a tidy legacy, and she suddenly found herself prey to the artful machinations of marriage-minded gentlemen searching for an heiress.

In the past, Percy had kept such suitors at bay, knowing that Mirabella would marry when and if she chose to do so. He'd never pushed or prodded her, and Mirabella had loved him all the more for such gentle understanding.

But suddenly Percy was gone. Her father's unexpected demise—and the many suitors cropping up to plague her—prompted Mirabella to travel abroad in the hopes of regaining the happiness she'd known during her father's lifetime.

As it was, neither time nor distance could heal her heart, and even in faraway Bengal, she had been plagued by several obnoxious suitors who had managed to tug the overextended purse strings of their benefactors and follow her into the jungle.

Now, standing in the lovely early-morning light, Mirabella sternly reminded herself that she hadn't returned to Stormhaven to remember but rather to

The Unmatchable Miss Mirabella   3

forget. So thinking, she lifted her silk hem and traipsed through the wet dew, heading straight for Annie, her favorite of Penelope's maids.

Annie was down on all fours, her rounded bottom propped into the air and her ear pressed to the ground beneath a hedge.

"Listen well, Max!" Annie said in a harsh whisper to the thick hedge. "Yer mistress will be spittin' nails when she wakes and finds yer not in 'er bed lickin' 'er toes! She'll 'ave me bleedin' arse in a sling, she will!"

"Looking for someone?" Mirabella asked, bending down beside Annie.

Annie didn't glance up. "Awk!" she said in that high-pitched voice of hers. "Would I be down on me bleedin' knees and talkin' to a hedge if I weren't?"

"One would hope not," Mirabella agreed reasonably. "Perhaps I could be of more assistance if you described this Max to me," she said.

"Big eyes. Fat. And lots of 'air!" came Annie's agitated reply. "And ooh, is 'e dumb," she added, poking around in the hedge with a stick. "Dumbest beast I ever did meet! Makes not a bit o' sense t' me why that dreamy Duchess of Ravenscar bothers t' let 'im warm 'er bed at night. True, the duchess swears 'e gives a good kiss t' 'er lily-white toes every evenin' afore she drifts off t' sleep, but is that any reason t' 'ave the likes o' Max makin' a mess in me kitchens or pawin' at me own skirts?"

Mirabella decided she'd best take the girl to task before she heard more about this Max and his obviously waggish ways.

"Really, Annie," said Mirabella, "I don't think you should be maligning one of Penelope's houseguests. And if this, er, Max is good *ton*, then I daresay you should take care in what you say about him."

"Good *ton*?" Annie screeched. "Are you addled? Max is a bleedin' *dog!*" So saying, she dropped her stick and pulled her head out of the hedge. She came up sputtering, mobcap askew and bouncy red curls littered with sticks. She blew a cobweb from her lips and gasped.

"La! Miss Bella! Is it really you?"

Mirabella laughed. "Yes, Annie. It is truly me. Surely you recognized my voice."

"I thought you was young Meg come t' devil me. Lawks, Miss Bella, but you've been gone this age, I vow!"

"I haven't been away that long, have I?"

"Thirteen months and one 'ellish sennight," replied Annie with faultless precision. "Last we 'eard, you was smugglin' thieves over some faraway border."

Mirabella felt a moment's guilt for not having kept in better touch with her eccentric godmama. Her smuggling adventure had taken place months ago—give or take the few weeks she'd spent nursing an ailing and cantankerous camel across the desert. She'd saved the camel, only to lose the letters she'd penned to Penelope in a duststorm.

"They were slaves, Annie. Turkish slaves," explained Mirabella patiently. "I was leading them to their freedom. Pity I didn't realize then that in their culture there is all manner of undying loyalty wafting about. Didn't my godmama tell you that I now have an overzealous Turk trailing me about? I am certain I wrote her of the fact. Indeed, I know I did, because I explicitly begged her to share with me her own secrets of taming a spitting camel."

"No, she didn't tell me," said Annie, wholly uninterested in the fact that Mirabella had been forced to deal with a moody camel, dine on odd dishes, and had very nearly been prompted to face Mecca numerous times a day for prayer along with all the other travelers.

Annie narrowed one green eye. "You didn't 'appen t' spy a King Charles spaniel named Max runnin' free an' peein' on every bush, did you, Miss Bella?"

Mirabella, giving up all hope of enlightening Annie as to her trials of the past months, shook her blonde head.

"Well, that leaves me in a pickle, it does," muttered Annie. "But enough o' me troubles." She rose to her feet, not bothering to dust off her dirt-smudged apron. "I be much more interested in what yer doin' 'ere, all trussed up in such threads. La, Miss Bella, but you look a might bit queer! 'As the fashions changed in London, or 'ave you lost yer baggage again?"

"The latter, I am afraid," Mirabella confessed.

There was no point in avoiding the issue, or of pointing out to the uninformed Annie that the Chinese silks she wore, along with the exotic satin slippers and the hammered gold earrings in her newly pierced ears, were all the rage . . . in Bengal.

The sorry fact was that Mirabella had lost her luggage. Again. Such seemed to be a regular occurrence with her. No matter how carefully she oversaw the packing of her trunks, or how often she checked and rechecked the various points of destination for her belongings, her plans always went awry. What mattered at the moment was that clearly, neither Mirabella's missive to her godmama announcing her imminent visit, nor her cloaked cage with its precious cargo, had arrived at Stormhaven.

"I wrote Aunt Nellie some time ago that I'd be arriving this week," said Mirabella, using her pet name for her godmama. "But come to think of it," she mused, half to herself, "I did leave the note in the hands of a harried sea captain who was most concerned with dealing with a band of pirates haunting the Thames. Said he could handle them and see that my belongings reached Stormhaven safely. The man assured me he was an expert with cutthroats and vagabonds, having been both at various points in his long life."

Annie nodded knowingly. "All river cap'ns are the same. Full o' lust and long legends! I wouldn't trust a one of 'em. Oh, la, Miss Bella!" she scolded. "You've lost yer touch, you 'ave. Since when do you trust a river cap'n?"

"Since I've learned to deal with fey desert princes," replied Mirabella. "So Aunt Nellie has no inkling of my arrival?"

"Not a whisper," said Annie.

"And my baggage?" Mirabella asked, somewhat desperate. "You're certain it hasn't arrived?"

Annie shook her head, her oversized mobcap whipping back and forth. " 'Aven't seen it. 'Course that don't mean it 'asn't arrived. Like I said 'afore, the last days 'ave been 'ellish indeed."

Annie leaned close to Mirabella, her voice dropping to a conspiratorial whisper. "There be a phantom runnin' loose, Miss Bella!"

"A phantom?" repeated Mirabella calmly. She wasn't surprised. The last time she'd visited, Annie had sworn she'd spied a headless ghost sitting atop the old stone wall down near the church. Claimed the ghost was waiting for the midnight coach.

"Annie," said Mirabella gently, "you haven't been dipping into Aunt Nellie's gin again, have you?"

"O' course I 'ave!" Annie sniffed. " 'Ow else could a girl face the likes o' the phantom? I saw it, too! Twice," she added, not without pride. "First time I seen it runnin' after the sheep. It was in animal form that time. Next night, I spied it sneakin' from that queer waterin' place yer godmama likes so much. 'E was in 'uman form that time. All 'andsome and near-naked with not a stitch o' clothin' on, only a sheet wrapped about 'im. La, but 'e was a glorious sight! All muscled and manly..." Annie closed her eyes, nearly swooning at the memory.

Mirabella hid a smile. Annie had spent the first part of her young life dodging the law and living on gin and whatever tidbits she could pilfer from the many chophouses in Town before Penelope, ever a merciful angel, plucked the girl from the streets and whisked her to the Cotswolds. Though Annie now worked in the cavernous kitchens of Stormhaven and seemed reformed, she still harbored a penchant for sneaking sweetmeats and stealing a sip or three from Penelope's store of gin.

The levelheaded Mirabella deduced that Annie probably hadn't spied a sheet-clad phantom at all, but rather one of her godmama's eccentric houseguests leaving Penelope's invigorating bathhouse, which was secluded on a hill behind the main house. As for the animal Annie had spied chasing sheep ...

"Tell me about this phantom," urged Mirabella.

"I just did! 'Andsome as a god. Pure man, 'e was, what with that shock of black 'air and all."

"I mean the beastly phantom," Mirabella said.

"Oh, that. Gruesome, 'e was." Annie shivered dramatically. "All fangs and claws. And such a sound! 'Owled at the moon, it did. And I swears it ate the Duchess o' Ravenscar's nuisance of a dog Max. That's why I'm pokin' around in this 'ere hedge. Not that I'll find poor Max. I believe 'e's gone as gone can be."

Annie dug into the pocket of her apron and produced a somewhat mangled diamond-studded collar.

"See?" she said. "That phantom ate poor Max! I found 'is collar in the gardens near the fountain. There'll be 'ell to pay when the duchess realizes 'er Max is dead!"

Mirabella stared down at the mangled collar, spying a familiar set of teeth marks.

Oh Zeus and Minerva! she thought. It wasn't a phantom Annie had spied chasing after Aunt Nellie's Cotswold sheep, but Mirabella's own tiger cub. It seemed her baggage had arrived after all. And someone, blast them, had freed the spaniel-eating Sasha from her cloaked cage.

Mirabella, not wanting to alarm Annie, calmly took the much-disfigured collar from the girl's hands. "I think you'd best call off the search for Max," she said.

"So you know where he is?"

"I believe I have an idea, yes."

"You do?" cooed Annie. "Oh, do tell! I don't want me ears boxed by that dreamy duchess. She 'as such a temper, y'know. Max was 'er pride and joy, and it was me own duty t' keep the dog in sight. She'll see me sent back t' the streets o' Covent Gard'n, she will, if Max isn't pantin' on 'er bed at noon today!"

Mirabella's fair brow wrinkled. She certainly didn't want to see the sweet Annie sent back to a life in the alleyways. Nor did she relish an uproar from one of her godmama's houseguests. As Mirabella saw it, she was obligated to find a replacement for one errant spaniel.

"I'll have Max returned here by noon. Is that good enough?"

"Oh, yes! But 'ow will you find that bleedin' nuisance if 'e's dead?"

Mirabella had no idea. She only knew she had

to replace one fat and furry spaniel before the clock struck twelve. Surely, in all the Cotswolds, there must reside another black-eyed creature that would be more than happy to curl up beside a duchess and lick her toes.

"Not to worry, Annie," said Mirabella, glad, in truth, to have a mission to keep her thoughts from the affairs that had led her to seek comfort beneath her godmama's protective wing. "I'll do my best to make things right as rain. Now, before I begin, I need a detailed description of Max."

Annie complied at length, then heaved a grateful sigh. "La, but I be glad yer 'ere, Miss Bella. You always could calm a storm. And I'll sleep better knowin' yer 'ere t' 'elp fend off that beastly phantom! As sure as I'm standin', you'll find a way t' trap that wily beast. As for its 'uman form, why, 'e'll take one look at you and swoon in 'is tracks, 'e will! 'E'll forget all about 'aunting these lands once 'e spies you."

Mirabella clicked her tongue. "Really, Annie, if I didn't know better, I'd swear you were resorting to your age-old scheme of trying to pair me off with a man, be he phantom or not."

"Well, seein' as 'ow you 'aven't fancied all the fine gents that 'ave offered for you o'er the years, mayhap you'll find favor in a phantom. 'E be odd and mysterious. Just yer cup o' tea."

"I haven't returned to Stormhaven to find a husband," Mirabella said with singular strength. "I've come for rest and relaxation—both of which I intend to pursue with vigor."

Annie smiled knowingly. "You say that now, but I be thinkin' you'll sing a different tune once you spy that 'andsome phantom. If there be any man t' turn yer thoughts t' love and marriage, it be 'im, Miss Bella, I do swear."

With that, Annie bustled away, calling to her fellow maids and leading the way back to the house.

Mirabella watched them retreat, wondering why in the devil she felt as though she had been tossed from the frying pan into the fire. She had come to Stormhaven for comfort, not chaos. And yet, in a matter of moments, she had found that her naughty Sasha had eaten a spaniel, Annie was set on a wild course of finding her an ideal *parti*, and some fair-of-face nodcock was wandering the grounds clad like a Roman gladiator!

Deciding that her wisest course of action was to meet each of the obstacles straight on, Mirabella headed back to her carriage and set her mind to the task of finding a spaniel who might be sweet enough, or dumb enough, to heel to the name of Max. She told herself that Sasha, her errant tiger cub, would most likely find a cool spot to slumber now that dawn had come, and wouldn't, she hoped, decide to trouble her godmama's sheep until nightfall. As Mirabella figured it, she had several hours before she need begin worrying about Sasha's prowling ... not to mention a handsome phantom haunting the lands.

Mirabella, her quick mind all agog with the many tasks she must accomplish this day, gave orders to her coachmen to hurry her to the nearest fair. Since the gentle Cotswolds countryside was full of them at this time of year, there should be one close-by.

Not only did her livery snap to life, but so did Haluk, one of the Turkish slaves she'd helped lead to freedom. He was a strapping fellow, tall and broad, with muscle upon muscle rippling down his huge chest. His eyes were a soft brown, his complexion dark and unmarred, and his mouth full and mobile. He wore his shoulder-length brown hair tied back in a thong, and had a disconcerting habit of appearing bare-chested in public.

At first Mirabella had worried about Haluk because he'd been wracked by fever for several days following their successful escape over the Turkish border. He'd snapped out of his delirium after a dreadful forty-eight hours, had taken one look at Mirabella's blue eyes and bright hair, and had instantly sworn himself her loyal follower for life. No matter what she said, she could not sway the handsome young man from his vow.

She'd tried unsuccessfully to dodge his watchful eye and leave him with his friends, but he had pursued her. Like an unwanted penny, he kept returning to the purse and had popped up on board her ship headed for England. Haluk insisted that since Mirabella had saved his life, he would return the favor by serving her for the remainder of his days. Considering that he was all of nineteen, that would doubtless prove to be a deuced *long* time.

The vessel on which they'd sailed had already been too far out to sea for Mirabella to do anything but resign herself to the fact that Haluk would accompany her back to England. Now that they'd reached Stormhaven, Mirabella hoped that Haluk would find new friends and make a home for himself within the odd household.

It was on the tip of Mirabella's tongue to gently order Haluk to remain behind. But he peered at her with such rapt loyalty and unspoken excitement in his warm brown eyes that she decided to keep her mouth shut. Who was she to dash his fun? His was a generous and open heart, and from the moment she'd met him, Mirabella had sensed in him a thirst to view the world. She could not be so unkind as to cheat Haluk out of a visit to a Cotswold fair! She bade him to ride on the hind boot.

Flashing her a wide grin, and bowing before her in a deep genuflection, Haluk assured his mistress that he wished to run alongside her carriage to protect her from harm.

"We are now in England, Haluk," Mirabella patiently explained. "There is no need to be so wary. My coachmen will see to my safety."

He harrumphed noisily, eyeing her well-dressed coachmen with barely concealed doubt. He thumped one balled fist against his chest. "Haluk will guard Miss Bella."

With a sigh, Mirabella waved at Haluk to do whatever it was he wished to do (Lord knew there was no use in arguing with him) and then allowed herself to be helped into her conveyance. She placed Max's collar on the seat beside her and tried not to think about the poor dead pup. In another moment, the carriage lurched forward, the tired horses heading down the graveled drive.

And so it was that Miss Mirabella Lavinia Darlington, late of tiger-sketching in Bengal, preceded by a strapping, bare-chested Turk who proudly carried two casks of jewels which had been given to Mirabella by a sultan she'd aided during a sandstorm, and she herself dressed in queer fashion, arrived at the sleepy town of Stow-on-the-Wold.

Who would have guessed she had come only to purchase a spaniel?

2

At a country fair just outside of Stow, Christian Phillip Edward White, the new Earl of Blackwood, tossed his offending rosewood cane to the ground and knelt down to ruffle the fur of a King Charles spaniel pup.

He ignored the pain that shot through his left thigh. *Damn the war*, his lordship thought to himself. And damn the French ball of lead that had buried itself in his thigh and subsequently made his life a living hell. The only thing that kept him from gritting his teeth in pain was the fact that come midnight, he would find himself alone amid the healing spa waters of his good friend Penelope Barrington's bathhouse.

Of course, traipsing across the English countryside shortly after dawn in search of a King Charles spaniel hadn't been his own choice. His lordship would have much preferred spending his morning hours alone in Penelope's secluded guest house, reading a copy of a several-days'-old *Gazette*.

But only this morning the lovable but outrageous Penelope had come calling, puffing on that ridiculous pipe of hers and muttering some nonsense about making the dreadful mistake of freeing a tiger from its cage. It seemed this tiger had done a most unforgivable thing—it had devoured the Duchess of Ravenscar's spaniel, and would Christian be a dear and go a-hunting for "poor Max's double?"

Blackwood, a gentleman and very much a champion of the eccentric but kindhearted Penelope, was obliged to come to the aid of his hostess. And so here he was down on bended, tricky knee, ruffling the ears of a dewy-eyed spaniel.

The pup seemed rather to like Blackwood's attentions, for it wagged its tail so forcefully that its round little rump bumped against Blackwood's healthy leg. A moment later, it bounded up on its back legs and gave his lordship several wet kisses.

Blackwood was instantly smitten. He nearly made an offer for the pup—until he spied a telltale patch of white beneath its furry neck. Dash it all! His search, alas, was far from over.

The earl cast his dark eyes about, seeking among the brood a suitable match to the Duchess of Ravenscar's Max.

The breeder of the spaniels, a noxious fellow and a seasoned hawker, ran one hand through his thinning, ill-kempt hair. "Oi have another litter comin', yer lordship, if you don't find a suitable one in this bunch. 'Course it won't be fer anuther six weeks. Oi be comin' back through in August."

"That won't do," said Blackwood. "I need a wavy-haired beast by noon today. And one without a smidgen of white."

Even as he said the words, Blackwood spied a round-bellied, perfectly black-and-brown puppy darting off toward a nearby Gypsy caravan.

"What about that one?" he said, motioning to the pup, who was squeezing its fat little body between the stout legs of a Gypsy.

"Eh? Oh! That be me own pet," said the man slyly. "It's captured me heart, it has. Oi wouldn't part with it, ever."

"Indeed?" said Blackwood, not at all convinced. "Name your price, man."

"Me price?" The man's rheumy eyes gleamed. "Yes, well ... Ahem! ... Yer not the first to offer fer that pup. Oi've had many offers this day, all most pleasin'."

"I'll match them," said his lordship crisply.

The man's jaw fell open, then snapped shut just as quickly. He obviously realized he had a famous sale all sewed up, right and tight, yet he knew better than to appear too eager.

"Hmmm, that be a fine offer, yer lordship, but like 'Oi said, there be others interested in this fine animal that has managed to steal me heart."

"Dash it all," grumbled Blackwood, not about to spend his entire morning haggling over the price of one King Charles spaniel that might—or might not—find a place in the Duchess of Ravenscar's bedchamber, "I'll double the highest offer you've had!"

"Double?" the seller croaked, taken by surprise. Lady Luck was indeed smiling upon him this day. He very nearly rubbed his hands together in wicked glee, but stopped short of doing so when he saw the look of dark intent upon the earl's face. He cleared his raspy throat. "Oi dunno," he said, hedging, hoping for an even higher offer. "That be a special pup, a right bonny descendant from King Charles's own—"

"Aren't they all?" his lordship cut in. "Just name your price and be quick about it."

The foul-smelling dog breeder was only too eager to oblige.

Blackwood frowned at finding himself being robbed of too many pence, but told himself it was of little consequence. If the spaniel came when called by the duchess, that was all that mattered.

"Sold," said Blackwood, motioning to his manservant, Haskins, to take care of the monetary transaction.

Without another glance behind him, Blackwood headed for the caravan ... and the pup that had, quick as lightning, disappeared beneath the flap of a brightly colored tent.

The chase was on.

Not bothering to await Haskins's assistance, Blackwood inquired of a robust Gypsy woman if he might have permission to enter the tent in search of his mischievous pup.

The woman took one look at Blackwood's handsome person and sent a fetching smile his way. Hands on rounded hips, she batted long, dark lashes up at him, and told him in a throaty voice that he could sleep in the tent if that was his wish.

Blackwood flashed the woman his famous grin, a smile that had, once upon a time, melted the heart of many a London lady.

He'd no sooner pulled up the flap of the tent and stepped through the opening than he came smack-dab against a soft and pliant figure.

"Oh!" exclaimed a sweet, feminine voice.

Blackwood peered into the darkness. "Excuse me," he blustered, not at all happy about having to scurry after some untrained mutt.

"Well, yes, I suppose I shall excuse you," came the cultured voice, "but really, you should take more care when stealing inside a tent."

"Stealing?" his lordship replied, somewhat miffed.

Fancy some chit claiming he was stealing anywhere! His leg felt on fire, not to mention the fact that he'd visited three fairs since dawn and not one of them had harbored a King Charles spaniel. Damnation, but this day was becoming intolerable!

"I have every right to bound through this tent," he told the mysterious female.

"On the contrary, sir," the woman replied, "I gave very precise orders that I did not want anyone entering this tent. I am on a mission. It is imperative that I not be disturbed."

"Oh?" he inquired, his curiosity piqued.

She had a lovely voice—one that, Blackwood was certain, would prove far lovelier when she was not in such a state of agitation.

The enchanting sound of it caused Blackwood to momentarily forget about tracking down the wayward pup. He allowed himself a moment to adjust to the absence of light. Very slowly, the wondrous sight of her came into view.

Blazes, but she was gorgeous. Blackwood noticed the lady's lovely eyes first. Summery-blue, they were, and fringed with thick, dusky lashes. Eyes to turn a man's head, surely; her steady gaze hinted she was nobody's fool. Her heart-shaped face and very pleasing features were framed by a mass of somewhat tousled and breathtakingly beautiful blonde curls. Her mouth was a perfect Cupid's bow of pouty pink.

But her mode of dress—what a queer rig!

She was outfitted in voluminous watered silks, bright in color and obviously from some Far Eastern bazaar. Blackwood, having traveled extensively on the Continent and beyond during his Grand Tour, noticed she wore a pair of gold Moorish slippers that peeked from under the sumptuous gown. He also noticed that the lobes of her prettily shaped ears were pierced not once, but thrice.

A most becoming but odd-looking miss. Blackwood wondered at her purpose at the fair, and how she'd come to be in the tent at such an uncivilized hour.

"A mission, eh?" he asked, suddenly feeling an overpowering urge to prolong their meeting.

"Yes, that is precisely what I said."

She blew out a sigh, casting a furtive glance toward the shadowy corners of the tent, as though searching for someone or something.

"I am looking for a ... a companion, you see," she continued. "It is imperative that I not be disturbed."

"And I have disturbed you. Forgive me."

Christian swept a low bow, giving her a handsome smile as he righted himself. "It seems we have something in common, after all."

His statement was met by a suspicious lifting of her fair brows.

"Allow me to explain," he added quickly. "I, too, am in search of a companion—so to speak."

Mirabella, who a scant second ago had mentally cursed at being interrupted in her attempt to lure the spaniel she'd bought into her arms, found herself mesmerized by the enigmatic man standing before her.

He was the epitome of fashion. He wore a coat of black superfine (Weston-made, undoubtedly), a properly creaseless Oriental, highly polished Hessians, and dark, skintight inexpressibles that showed to advantage his long and muscled legs. And if that were not enough to turn a lady's glance his way, he had a heavy shock of black hair that tumbled romantically over his forehead.

Mirabella was transfixed by the sight of him. Everything about him spoke of privilege and breeding. And though she was neither a young miss fresh from the schoolroom, nor a wily, husband-hunting debutante of the *ton*, she realized she didn't want him to dash away.

"I say," he offered, "if you share your secrets of

what type of companion you seek, I shall share mine. Perhaps we might be of assistance to each other."

Was he being flirtatious, or serious? Mirabella couldn't be certain. She was already in high fidgets. "The companion I seek is, uh, very reckless," she said, "and obviously one who travels his own road in life."

"Amazing," replied the man with rapt attention. "So too is mine."

Mirabella smiled. He was very handsome. And though he'd seemed a bit testy when he first spoke, he appeared to be the supreme gentleman now. Her smile warmed.

"The companion I seek is very particular in choosing his acquaintances. Very particular indeed," she said.

"Ah! So this chosen companion shall not be led by the nose, eh? Nothing done just for the sake of propriety."

"Oh, no, none of that."

"Famous! Just the sort of companion I am in search of. What else, fair lady?"

Mirabella felt a blush suffuse her cheeks. How silly of her. She was talking about the type of pup she needed to acquire, and not the sort of man with whom she actually hoped to share a lifetime . . . wasn't she?

Suddenly, she found herself plunging headlong into the game, erecting in her own mind the perfect *parti* she hoped to find one day. Words flowed from her lips.

"This companion shall be strong, yet harbor a soft and loving soul."

"Definitely a loving soul."

"And be committed," she added.

"Ah, yes. A sense of commitment is paramount." He paused momentarily. "But be committed to what? The church? The state?"

"Family first," she said without hesitation.

"Yes," he agreed, eyeing her closely. "Family first."

"But he shall have the heart of a corsair." She was caught up in the game. "He shall be unafraid to take to the waters of life. He shall harbor a bold heart that does not balk at the threat of choppy seas."

"Precisely what I seek," said the handsome gentlemen. "A woman who opens her arms to her loving corsair, and who is unafraid of embarking on roads less traveled. A woman who knows that to embrace life is to live it to its fullest!"

"A man who sees the beauty in a sunrise," continued Mirabella, letting her eyes drift shut in dreamy wonder and seeing again the sun rise over a faraway desert. She thought, too, of all the star-filled nights she'd witnessed on that same desert. Her heart quickened.

Blackwood, taken by the woman's intensity, stared at the dusky shadows cast upon her high cheekbones by her long lashes.

Throatily, he whispered, "I seek a woman who finds hope in the night ... a woman who can perceive promise amid the broken stars that scar a night sky."

Mirabella snapped her eyes open. Their innocent game had turned suddenly serious ... and mayhap even a tad risqué.

"Forgive me, sir, but I fear I've misled you. I am searching for a—"

She never finished her sentence.

The moment was shattered when a markedly handsome Gypsy stepped inside the tent—the same man to whom Mirabella had paid a handsome sum to ensure that no one entered the tent while she was trying to coax into her arms the nervous pup she'd purchased.

"I am Tomislav Karoly Jozsef Vilaghy! I am in love with you! Prepare to fall equally in love with me!" he announced.

The intruder threw his handsome physique down on bended knee, clasping one hand to his heart in a poetic, romantic gesture.

Mirabella gaped at the Gypsy with wide eyes. Zeus and Minerva! Whatever had prompted the man to follow her inside and make such a statement? Certainly she'd been kind to him, but not *that* kind.

"There is no need to kneel down before me," she told the Gypsy.

He jumped quickly to his feet, casting her a comely grin as he did so.

"Then I, Tomislav Karoly Jozsef Vilaghy, shall offer for you standing up!" he cried.

"No, no," said Mirabella. "I don't think you understand. There is no need to offer for me at all!"

"But I must!" said the Gypsy. "I have watched you from afar this morn, and I find you are all that I desire! We shall marry." He snapped his fingers in the air. "Yes, we shall! Soon. Today!"

"*Marriage?*" echoed Mirabella, taking a step back. "But I wish to marry no man!"

The Gypsy's grin widened appreciatively. "If it isn't marriage you seek, then I, Tomislav Karoly Jozsef Vilaghy, shall be an attentive lover! I shall take you places you have never been. I shall show you sights you have never seen ..."

Mirabella stared at the man in horror.

The gentleman near her leaned closer. "Could he be the companion you seek?" he whispered.

"Certainly not!"

"Very well, then." And to her complete dismay, he turned on the Gypsy with a stern look and said, "The lady is spoken for, my good man. Were I you, I would head out of this tent and forget the incident."

The Gypsy, however, did not immediately depart. "Spoken for? By whom?"

"By me," he announced.

"*You?*"

The single word was spoken in unison by both the lady and the lust-filled Gypsy. The lady's voice registered shocked dismay, the Gypsy's strong disbelief.

"You heard me aright," said Blackwood. "I have laid claim to the lady's heart." He skewered the Gypsy with a look he hoped was a proper hint to begone. Though his lordship had not intended to play noble knight to a damsel, he suddenly found himself thrust into the role. He could hardly leave the lady to her own devices. Claiming himself as her suitor seemed to Blackwood the wisest choice; one that would, he hoped, force the Gypsy to leave without causing a ruckus. "I intend to make her my wife," he added for good measure.

The lady sucked in a quick breath. "Sir," she whispered, "you needn't spin such a ridiculous tale."

"You would rather I escorted him bodily from the tent?" he asked, his voice low. "That can be arranged."

"Pray, do not! I—I have seen his brothers, sir . . . all six of them."

"That many, eh?"

She nodded, shuddering. "They appeared an unruly lot, I assure you."

Blackwood was not of a mind to face down a pack of irate Gypsy brothers. "Well, then, I suppose I shall continue playing the part of your suitor," he whispered. And he bestowed upon the lady a warm and private smile, making certain the Gypsy had full view of that smile.

Mirabella could not help the shiver that raced up her spine and directly radiated to her limbs, leaving her weak-kneed. She could feel the heat of his gaze as surely as if he'd touched her bare skin, and the way in which his sensual mouth curved into an intimate smiles nearly took the breath out of her.

She knew at once that this man, with his fathomless jet-black eyes and curious words of nights scarred by starlight, was unlike any of the gallants who had sought to make a match with her. This man would take what he wanted and would never suffer being denied. But to claim that he wished to *marry* her? The man was not serious, she knew; he was merely playing a part in an attempt to thwart the Gypsy. So why, thought Mirabella, was she reacting to his words, his gaze, like some lovestruck schoolgirl? She felt a deep flush of discomfiture. She lowered her lashes and looked away, lest he see how much he'd affected her.

Blackwood noted the lady's blush, the alarmed quickness with which she'd shuttered her gaze from him. He noted, too, how the Gypsy's eyes widened and then just as quickly narrowed shrewdly. Clearly, the man had some doubts as to whether or not the fair lady reciprocated Blackwood's affections. No matter. His lordship knew how to ensure that the Gypsy left the tent posthaste. Blackwood's idea hinged on the lady's reaction to his statement of desiring to make her his wife. She was actually beginning to tremble, and the pulse point at the base of her long and slender neck was beating rapidly. He'd done more than just surprised her with his words; he'd unnerved her, had caught her off guard. It wouldn't do at all to have her trembling like a leaf caught in a brisk wind.

Blackwood took a step nearer to the woman, his body flush with hers. "Look at me," he whispered.

"Ex-excuse me?"

"Look at me," he said again. He reached for her gloved hands, covered them with his own. She looked up. He grinned. "That's it. Now smile. Act enthusiastic. Entranced." He motioned toward the Gypsy with just a lifting of his brows. "You wish to have him gone, do you not, and peacefully at that?"

She nodded.

"Should be a simple thing, then." Blackwood entwined his fingers with hers. "Play that you are in love with me and I with you."

Mirabella felt the stabbing heat of him all the way to her toes. He was too close, the masculine scent of him suprisingly stimulating. Good Lord, what had she gotten herself into? Before she could pull away, the man lowered his head toward hers. He boldly brushed his lips across her mouth—a feathery-light touch intended only to fool the Gypsy. The contact of his lips upon hers, however, sent Mirabella's senses reeling. Lord, if this was how he kissed when acting a part, how might he kiss a woman when caught in the throes of passion? Not that it mattered. She would never allow the man near her again. How dare he take such liberties, she thought as he burned a hot trail to her ear. She felt the *swoosh* of his warm breath, and stiffened, forcing herself not to give in to a delicious tremor.

"I could be wrong," he whispered, "but I do believe that a woman in love would yield more to her lover's touch."

"I should slap you!" she said under her breath.

She felt his mouth curve into a grin against her skin. "Yes. But you won't."

"How can you be so certain?"

"Because if you do, your Gypsy friend will feel the need to come to your rescue. I haven't been involved in a brawl since my salad days at university, but I assure you, I haven't forgotten what I learned there."

Mirabella, too caught up in anger at his audacity and embarrassment at her own physical reaction to him, gave no heed to the man's warning. Instead, she yanked her hand from his hold and made a motion to push him away—a motion which he ignored.

The Gypsy seized that moment to cry, "Ha! I knew it to be so! The lady, she does not favor you! I, Tomislav Karoly Jozsef Vilaghy, must call you out, sir! Name your weapon!"

"Gadzooks," Blackwood muttered. He frowned at Mirabella. "I truly wish you hadn't pulled your hand from mine as though you'd been scorched. I was, after all, only trying to save you from your overzealous friend."

"He isn't my friend. I never met him until this morning," Mirabella snapped, her voice low.

"Does every man you encounter throw himself down on bended knee and propose to you?"

She did not deign to reply. If only he knew!

"Your weapon of choice, sir!" demanded the high-strung Gypsy.

Blackwood, his gaze firmly fixed on the maddening miss before him, felt his irritation toward the Gypsy mount. Bloody hell! He didn't for a moment believe that the man could best him either with swords or pistols. His lordship had been renowned for his swordplay (before his war injury, of course, though he had been training rigorously since then and was nearly up to snuff once again), and he was and always had been an excellent shot. He would certainly be the victor of any duel. Problem was, he'd had enough of warring to last him a lifetime.

"I wish you hadn't prompted matters to go this far," he muttered to the lady.

She had the nerve to stare up at him with incredulous eyes. "*Me?*" she sputtered. "Need I remind you, sir, that you were the one who initiated this foolish masquerade, not I!"

"Enough!" interrupted the Gypsy. "You will badger the lady no more! Name your weapon!"

Blackwood momentarily considered rounding on the irritating fellow and ending this absurd confrontation with a solid wisty castor to the man's jaw. But, of course, his lordship would do no such thing; he was a man of title and wealth, had been raised from the cradle to expect all the world to bend to his will, and had been reared to adhere to the precise rigors of genteel Society. Pity, then, that Society deemed a gentleman to be forever chivalrous where a lady was concerned.

"Oh, bother," said Blackwood. His eyes not leaving the woman's too-lovely face, he said over one shoulder to the Gypsy, "My choice is swords. Declare a date and time, you odious intruder."

The lady's face turned ashen. "This is madness!" she cried. "Do not say you intend to carry out this infamous duel!"

"I'd say the matter is already settled," Blackwood commented, noting how she trembled anew. For a woman who had at first seemed so worldly and independent, she now appeared quite unhinged. "Are you fretting over my welfare ... of your Gypsy's?"

Blackwood didn't get an answer, for the Gypsy interrupted them again, complaining about his lordship's choice of weapons. He crossed one arm about his chest, plopped his right arm atop it, and then reached up to cup his chin in his hand. "You are too hasty, perhaps, eh? Swords, they can be messy, no? All that nicking of the opponent!" He shivered with distaste. "Perhaps you should choose pistols, yes? I, Tomislav Karoly Jozsef Vilaghy, will see that we have the finest pistols with which to duel. I will shoot you dead, with one shot between the eyes, eh? No pain for you, no mess for me!" But then he fell into deep thought yet again. "But pistols, they can be just as messy, no? All that spurting blood from penetrating wounds ... and the noise! My ears, they ache at the thought! Perhaps swords would be best. Yes, choose swords! I shall draw first blood and then all will be settled. You will go your way, and I, Tomislav Karoly Jozsef Vilaghy, shall win the lady's heart. Simple, no?"

Oh, for the love of God, thought Blackwood. He eyed the lovely lady and whispered "You need only play that you are enamored of me and the Gypsy will be gone. He is, as he has just pointed out, trying to win your heart. Show him your heart is with me and he will desist, I am certain."

Mirabella thought better of the notion, but wished to have no blood shed over her favors. "There will be no need for a duel," she told the Gypsy, leaning toward the mysterious stranger. "I—I am quite enamored of—of my gentleman friend."

"I do not believe you!" cried the Gypsy.

Mirabella did her best to appear smitten with the black-eyed gentlemen. "It is true," she said, hating the lie that passed her lips, and hating even more her own involuntary shiver as her shoulder brushed the man's.

"This I cannot believe!"

"Believe it," replied the gentleman, his tone

brooking no argument as his left arm slipped about Mirabella's tiny waist.

She bit back a cry of outrage.

The Gypsy backed away. "If you insist, my precious lady," he murmured, bowing deeply toward her. "I, Tomislav Karoly Jozsef Vilaghy, would not dream of upsetting you." He straightened, flashing her a grin. "I come to you should you ever have need of me." To the stranger, he said, "You, sir, have not seen the last of Tomislav! We duel ... someday!" And then, blowing a kiss to Mirabella, the Gypsy backed out of the tent, leaving her alone with the assuming, arrogant gentleman.

Mirabella instantly stiffened. She debated whether or not to ring a peal over the man for so boldly bussing her mouth. She glared up at him, and in that instant when her gaze clashed with his unwavering jet-black eyes, she knew she would do no such thing. There was an air of authority and command about him, and she suddenly found the blue-blooded perfection of his features intimidating. She instinctively knew he was a man not to be reprimanded. Even though Mirabella had long thumbed her nose at authoritative figures, she was not of a mind to do so now. She was wrung out from her long journey home to Stormhaven and from her hectic search for a suitable substitute for Max. All she wanted at the moment was to find the spaniel and be on her way.

So thinking, she said, "I—I suppose I should thank you for saving me from an undesired encounter, sir."

"Of course." The man nodded obligingly. "Anything for a damsel in distress."

Mirabella felt her face grow hot. She did not care to be labeled as some damsel in distress—nor did she like the heady feeling stealing through her at the man's barest touch.

"Is that what you think of me?" she demanded, a bit harshly. Her harshness, of course, was borne of the plain fact that the gentleman had the uncanny ability to make her heart go all a-flutter. Mirabella's heart had *never* gone a-flutter in the presence of a man. She didn't like it. Not one bit.

"Well, yes," he answered "Most assuredly a damsel in distress."

"Hardly!" she replied, affronted. "I am rarely without my resources." She gazed up at him with unflinching blue eyes. "You may release me, sir. The danger is now past. I am quite capable of taking my own self out of this tent."

His lordship, having regained some of his good humor, tipped a grin at her. "But the question remains why you entered in the first place."

"I told you. I am on a mission."

"Oh, yes. That." He cast a glance about them. "And have you espied this, uh, companion?"

Mirabella gnashed her teeth. The man was obviously goading her, since they were the only two people in the tent. Of a sudden, she had a horrid thought: had he sensed the tripping of her heart and the catch of her breath as he'd touched her? Lord, she hoped not. It wouldn't do at all to have the rake believing he held some sway over her senses.

Mirabella saw a black shadow move in the corner to her left. Her spaniel. It must be.

"As a matter of fact," she told the man, "I have found my desired companion."

Mirabella saw the man's black eyes gleam appreciatively, noted how he leaned almost imperceptibly closer to her. Oh, but he was an accomplished seducer, she thought. She offered him a devastating smile, planning all the while how she might bring him down a peg or two.

Blackwood, meanwhile, found himself smitten

by the lady's beguiling smile. Christ's nails, but she had a way of narrowing her pretty eyes and making a man wonder what thoughts were teeming through her brain. In truth, he hadn't been so intrigued by a lady in ... well, not since before his war injury. Such a revelation was not only surprising, but also confusing.

Blackwood did not fancy becoming all doe-eyed by a queerly outfitted miss who haunted fairs. Surely he was addled by his own self-imposed solitude, he thought. He was simply out of the habit. Yes, that was it. He'd been too far gone from any dealings with the fairer sex.

"Well then," he said, "I suppose I should leave you to claim your companion, fair lady."

Even as he said the words, he wondered if she would bat her lovely lashes and demurely tell him he was the very one she sought. Truth be known, he expected such a reaction, as he'd received flirtatious advances by more than one lady scheming to make an advantageous match.

But this lady did no such thing.

Instead, she nodded once, dismissing him, and turned her attention to a pup scouting the corner of the tent in curiosity. She moved toward it with the utmost care. And dash it all, but she actually enticed the wayward spaniel into her arms with just a click of her tongue and some sweet, nonsensical words.

Clutching the pup to her breast, she turned toward him with a brilliantly happy smile.

"My mission is complete," she announced. "I have found my companion. Now, if you will excuse me?"

A stunned Blackwood stared in disbelief. Good Lord, she'd been talking of a dog all this time. And not just *any* dog.

The exotic miss was stealing his own pup from beneath his nose—the very spaniel for which he'd searched high and low, and for which he'd paid an outrageous price!

3

"I say, is something wrong, sir?" Mirabella inquired, fighting to hold on to the wiggling pup that was frantically trying to lick her face. The man standing before her seemed vexed. No doubt the cause of his vexation was none other than herself.

Mirabella realized it had been cruel of her to encourage the gentleman and give him cause to believe she might actually name him as her desired companion. She wouldn't have normally done such a beastly thing. But he'd seemed so cocksure of himself that Mirabella, mightily weary of blue-blooded gentlemen who made sport with the petticoat line, had found herself hard-pressed not to indulge in a harmless prank.

"You look a bit peaked," she said earnestly. "Could it be the musty air of this tent has got the best of you? Here. I'll open the flap. Let in some good air. You'll be right as rain in a moment, I'm sure—"

"No!" insisted Blackwood, eyeing the pup that was now eager to be away. "There's no need, I assure you!"

Too late.

The lovely lady no sooner pushed open the flap of the tent than the energetic spaniel leaped out of her arms. It landed with a thump on the grass and darted away, quick as a wink.

"Oh, Zeus and Minerva!" the lady muttered angrily.

"My thoughts exactly," rejoined Blackwood.

Together, they watched the pup race off into the main of the fairgrounds at breakneck speed. And then, as though hit by the same switch, they darted after the errant beast.

"Really, you needn't trouble yourself, sir!" the lady called. "It is my pup and my problem."

Blackwood set his jaw against the pain shooting up his left leg. He'd be damned if he'd allow a spaniel—or a lady in garish silks—to outrace him. As for her claim of ownership, that was another thing.

"No trouble, fair lady," he managed to call, and then, remembering her earlier pique, thought to add, "Anything for a damsel in distress!"

Mirabella ran faster. Damsel in distress, eh? She'd show him distress!

Ignoring the fact that she might very well make a cake of herself by careening through the fair, she picked up speed and outdistanced the man by several yards. A small smile touched her lips. She was enjoying their madcap race!

Trouble loomed ahead, however, in the form of a skirted dancing bear. The beast sported a wild creation for a hat that was heavily embellished with ribbons and huge, dyed feathers that fanned out in all directions.

Mirabella nimbly dodged the twirling bulk of fur and ridiculous feathers.

Her pursuer was not so fortunate.

She glanced back over one shoulder to see the stranger being waylaid by a cloud of feathers as the bear danced into his path and obscured his view.

"Zounds!" she heard the man exclaim.

She suppressed a giggle, for the sight of the

dashingly handsome man batting feathers from his nose and *ah-chooing* loudly was quite comical. Had she not a more pressing matter to attend, she might have lingered to enjoy the sight and even aid the man. But the pup was directly ahead, having paused to sniff the ground near a fruit stall.

Another few steps and she would have the spaniel in her hands.

The pup glanced up at her with devilish eyes and, apparently thinking Mirabella wanted to play, scooted its little rump to the side, cleverly avoiding her outstretched hands. It gave a happy yip, tail wagging as Mirabella nearly toppled over it. Silky ears cocked, the dog jumped over her gloved hands and scrambled round the side of the fruit stall.

"Drat!" said Mirabella, righting herself.

She scurried after it—and ran smack-dab into a long line of pigs being led by a weary farmer.

"Oh!"

Several frightened piglets entangled themselves in her skirts. There came much squealing and squawking as the piglets weaved a confused path around her. In another moment, she would be flat on her backside, and peering eye-level into their snouts!

"Steady now. I've got hold of you," said a low and very calming voice beside her.

Mirabella glanced up into the face of the obsidian-eyed gentleman she'd last seen tangling with a dancing bear. A lone pink feather clung to his otherwise impeccable coat.

"Pigs are like sheep, I fear," he said, gently guiding her back a step and out of harm's way. "They have a silly habit of playing follow-the-leader. Pity their leader chose to circle about you."

Held safely in his arms, Mirabella watched as the piglets dutifully fell back into line and commenced onward. They formed a frightfully long procession—long enough, that is, for her to feel the warmth of the man seeping into her flesh through their layers of clothing.

"You are not hurt, are you?" he inquired.

"I am quite all right," she insisted, feeling foolish. And guilty. "I am sorry I left you to deal with that skirted bear alone."

"No apology needed. I daresay I have taken to the dance floor with less sure-footed partners."

"But none adorned with so many feathers, I am certain."

"You are right about that!"

Suppressing a giggle, Mirabella motioned to the wilted pink feather clinging to his coat.

The man had to good grace to laugh. With a chuckle, he brushed the feather from his sleeve.

Mirabella liked the sound of his laughter. Perhaps she had misjudged him. Perhaps he wasn't as full of himself as she had first thought.

She found herself staring a mite too intently at the handsome lines of his aquiline face and then into the intriguing depths of his black eyes.

She should have known better than to look too closely, for what she saw muddled her mind and made her again feel, for a moment, like some lovestruck girl fresh from the schoolroom. Heavens, but the man was far too handsome for his own good—and for hers!

She gave herself a mental shake, deducing she was too travel-weary, and thus ill-prepared to be thrown into such close proximity with a gentleman who was clearly versed in the ways of seducing any female who chanced to cross his path. She studiously forced herself to take a step away from him.

Blackwood noted the lovely lady's sudden skittishness, but had noted, too, her curious and unabashed gaze a moment earlier. She was no shrinking violet. 'Twas a fact he both applauded and appreciated as he had no patience for simpering females. Thankfully, she hadn't fallen to pieces when he'd boldly kissed her in the tent (though Lord knew he'd obviously set her at sixes and sevens with such a deliberate move!), and she had handled herself admirably in the face of the Gypsy's fervent proposal. How refreshing to come upon a female who did not completely wilt at the slightest provocation. She appeared to be a miss capable of handling any situation.

Blackwood allowed himself a moment to enjoy the lady's nearness. The exotic scent of her filled his senses. No ordinary lavender or tame rosewater for this original miss! She smelled of the Far East, with all its mystic secrets, all its magic. Blackwood drew in a deep breath.

The memory of their stolen kiss, of the lady's soft, sweet mouth beneath his, caused a burst of unexpected pleasure to spread through him. He had stolen kisses in the past, certainly, but never had he been so affected by them. And the fact that he'd barely made use of his offensive walking stick during his madcap dash after the lady and the spaniel made him all the more pleased. At long last, his wound appeared to be finally healing.

He could not help but smile at the lady. If not for her, he wouldn't have raced with the wind and put his injured thigh to the test, nor would he have played knight errant to a damsel in distress.

Oh, Lord! thought Mirabella, seeing a too-handsome grin crease his face and reach all the way to his dark eyes. What a practiced flirt he was—and what a ninnyhammer she was in reacting to his smile! She was doing exactly what she'd vowed she would never do: she was melting like a thin April snow beneath his taunting and too-warm smile!

At that moment, the wayward spaniel retraced its steps and came running pell-mell toward Mirabella's legs.

Thank God! she thought.

Lightning-quick, she bent down and scooped up the pup.

"Finally, I have you!" she cried. "Oh, but what a perfect nuisance you have been! I warn you now you'll not be getting away from me again so easily. I've paid a fair price to take you home with me—and take you home I shall. This instant!"

Blackwood frowned. By God, but that thieving hawker had sold the pup not once, but twice! Dash it all, that did leave him in a fix.

Well, there was nothing to do but come out with it.

"Excuse me," he said, "but I am afraid there has been some mistake."

"Sir?"

"That pup is mine. I purchased the spaniel not twenty minutes ago."

The lovely lady's eyes widened, then just as quickly narrowed. Obviously, she wasn't about to relinquish ownership.

"Then I have outfoxed you by ten minutes, sir, for I purchased the pup well over thirty minutes past!"

"Touché," he said.

His lordship was pleased by her show of spunk, as too few ladies of the *ton* ever had a single thought of their own, much less the ability to speak such a thought outright. But he must take possession of that spaniel. His hostess would be most upset should he not return victorious from his mission, and a certain duchess would doubtless be slashing the curtains and biting off the heads of anyone within reach, should she not have a familiar-looking King Charles spaniel licking her toes come noon today.

"Forgive me," he said, "but I doubt you paid as exorbitant a sum as did I for this pup."

He rattled off the number of pence his manservant, Haskins, was doubtless still counting out for the dog breeder.

The lovely lady gasped. "You paid *that* much? Why, you are even more of a fool than I!"

Blackwood forced himself not to wince at her cutting remark. "No need to rub salt in the wound," he replied dryly.

"No, indeed," she said, far too quickly. "Especially since I have no intention of giving up this dog. I am sorry, sir, but I must have this spaniel. I *must*!"

She held the tiny dog aloft, wrinkling her pert and pretty nose as the pup happily lapped its tongue against the curve of her chin.

"You see?" said she. "He likes me. And I must profess that I have become unexpectedly fond of him in return."

Blackwood felt a perfect scoundrel. The lady had clearly taken a shine to the small beast. Who was he to spoil her happiness?

His heart warming, he watched as the tiny pup wriggled in her hands—and then, to his extreme relief, he espied a telling detail he had heretofore grossly overlooked.

Gadzooks! he thought, staring in the region of the pup's pot belly. This particular pup was not at all what he was searching for. He felt vast relief, glad he'd realized his mistake before he'd delivered the pup to one Duchess of Ravenscar. Only imagine the scandal had he done so!

His lordship tipped his beaver hat in the direction of the comely lady. "Do forgive me for being such a brute," he said congenially. "I had not realized the bond betwixt you and the pup. I bid you good day, fair lady," he said.

And he turned away, heading for Haskins and his coach.

He would have liked to have found some reason to linger in the lovely lady's company. What with her spunk and her outspoken ways, this particular female was, well, rather endearing. He couldn't put a finger on exactly what else it was about her that intrigued him. The urge to stay and chat with her was both tempting and inexplicable.

Nevertheless, he reminded himself sternly, he must whisk himself off to yet another fair in search of a perfect King Charles spaniel to grace the bed of the Duchess of Ravenscar. *Ah, Penelope,* he thought, *but you have no idea of the sacrifices I have made for you this day!*

"Sir?" called the lady.

Blackwood paused and turned. "Yes?"

"Thank you," she said simply.

"For what?"

"For not pressing your advantage and arguing over ownership of this pup, of course."

"Of course," he said, and again he tipped his hat her way. "You are quite welcome."

He would not sully the moment by revealing that the pup was, after all, not in the least what he'd been searching for. It left a bitter taste in his mouth to know that should the pup have been all "poor Max" was, he would have indeed pressed his advantage.

He rather liked being thought of as a champion. God knew he hadn't been a champion on the battlefield, for if he had, he would not have returned to England with a lame leg and a passel of horrid memories. And if he had been any sort of a champion, he would have managed a way to save his beloved brother's life and that of a certain lady as well.

The war had been won without him.

And his brother and the lady, both so very, very dear to him, had died tragic deaths.

Blackwood's thoughts turned suddenly dark. Abruptly, he turned on his heel.

He did not notice that the lady gazed after him curiously. Nor did he notice that the pup, once so frisky, lowered its ears and whimpered softly at his retreat.

4

Mirabella watched as the handsome devil who had kissed her and unnerved her headed away. Shaken to the core, she looked in the opposite direction and saw Haluk hastening toward her.

"Miss Bella!" he exclaimed. "Is there trouble? Haluk looked for you in the tent, but you were gone!"

Mirabella forced a smile, hoping to reassure him. "I am fine, Haluk. Look, I have found the spaniel we came in search of. Our mission is complete. We shall hurry back to Stormhaven."

"You are certain there is no trouble?" Haluk asked, obviously not convinced.

Mirabella waved away his concern, fighting to control the heat spreading across her cheeks. So the gentleman had kissed her—what of it? He'd wished to see the Gypsy gone. That was all. And the only reason the man had raced after her through the fair was because he'd purchased the same spaniel she had. It was pure foolishness to think the man's kiss meant anything more. But as Mirabella led Haluk back to the carriage, and as the conveyance lurched over the uneven country roads, she couldn't help but recall the whispery softness of the gentleman's mouth upon hers, and later his warm arms encircling her as he'd guided her safely away from the long line of pigs that had become entangled in her skirts.

Mirabella's mind was still filled with thoughts of the man when the carriage came to a halt on the graveled drive of her godmama's home. Haluk, having set down the two casks of jewels he'd borne to the fair and back again, rushed forward. Even before her coachmen had a chance to do so, Haluk popped open the door and let down the carriage steps. Mirabella's livery frowned in disapproval as Haluk made a great show of guiding their mistress out of the conveyance. He preened like a proud lion, clearly pleased with himself.

Not to be outshone by the Turk, the youngest of the coachmen, red-haired Henry, seized the opportunity to scoop up Mirabella's playful pup and the mangled collar as well. "Miss Darlington!" he said, snapping to attention before her—and shouldering Haluk to one side. "I shall personally take care of your new pet, if that pleases you!" He gazed at her with woefully concealed adoration.

Mirabella inwardly groaned; she'd had quite enough of besotted menfolk. "Thank you, Henry, but no, that won't be necessary. I shall take the dog and the collar. Do see to the horses and the few parcels I've brought with me."

"Oh, yes, Miss Darlington!" Henry gave over the wriggling spaniel and collar. He blushed furiously to the roots of his red hair when his gloved hand accidentally brushed against Mirabella's.

Haluk harrumphed noisily, giving a warning glare to the young coachman, which Henry pointedly ignored. Mirabella feared to two might resort to fisticuffs over her attentions. She gently ordered Henry to see to his duties, a command which he obeyed, though not without sending one last withering look in Haluk's direction. Haluk's lips twisted into a grimace of dislike.

Mirabella spied Annie heading toward them.

She motioned for the maid, and Haluk momentarily took his gaze off Henry.

"Ah," cried Annie at sight of the spaniel, " 'tis Max! Though a bit younger than the original, 'tis a fine replacement t' be sure!"

Mirabella felt a moment of relief. Perhaps her purchase—and the kiss she'd suffered at the hands of the gentleman—would not be in vain, after all. "Has the duchess arisen?" she asked.

Annie wasn't listening; she had eyes only for the bare-chested Haluk. "La," she whispered to Mirabella in a low voice, "did you find 'im at the fair as well, Miss Bella? Coo, but 'e is ever so 'andsome."

Mirabella clicked her tongue in exasperation. Here was another new worry. Would nothing prove simple this day?

"Annie," said Mirabella, her patience wearing thin, "has the duchess arisen or not?"

"Oh, she be risen, Miss Bella. The duchess, she likes t' perch 'erself beside the fountain in the gardens, she does. She be there now, cryin' in her kerchief and mutterin' 'bout the loss of 'er Max," said Annie.

"Famous," mumbled Mirabella, not at all pleased with the news.

Annie was too busy batting her eyelashes at Haluk to notice.

Haluk paid the maid not a bit of attention. He was too caught up in watching Henry carry Mirabella's parcels. Haluk gave a grunt of outrage when the young coachman made a motion toward the casks of priceless jewels. "Touch those and Haluk will be forced to cut your head from your body!" the Turk warned.

"Haluk!" scolded Mirabella. "We are in England now. There will be no severing of anyone's head. Pray remember that."

Haluk immediately backed down. Quietly he said, "Haluk, and only Haluk, will guard Miss Bella's jewels."

"Yes, yes," said Mirabella, "and so you shall." She motioned Henry and his fellow coachmen to take the carriage round the house to the stables, where they would unload the rest of her possessions in peace. She instructed Haluk to follow Annie inside the manor. "Annie will show you to your quarters, Haluk."

"And the jewels?" Annie muttered, her eyes glazing over with amazement as she espied the heavy casks that the young Turk lifted with ease onto his shoulders.

"Haluk will safeguard them, I am certain," said Mirabella.

"But who will safeguard *'im?*" Annie breathed. "Ain't every day a man walks bare-chested round Stormhaven, Miss Bella!"

Mirabella sent the maid a stern look. "Show Haluk inside, Annie. I would, of course, be ever so grateful if you would see to it that Haluk has some proper threads to don. A shirt would do nicely."

"And cover up that fine chest? Are you sure, Miss Bella?" the maid whispered.

"I am very sure, Annie."

"If you say so, Miss Bella." Annie gave a toss of her bouncy curls, then nodded toward the house, motioning the broad-shouldered Turk to follow her. Haluk, balancing the casks, trailed behind.

Mirabella heaved a sigh of relief. Now, all she had to do was deliver the counterfeit Max to a fretting duchess and, assuming the Duchess of Ravenscar didn't cry foul play, Mirabella would be free to do exactly as she had planned to do on this trip home: she would finally come to grips with her father's demise, and try to make some sense of her topsy-turvy life. Of course, there were also the tasks of finding Sasha, her errant tiger cub, and determining if there was indeed a phantom prowling the grounds of Stormhaven. But everything in good time, Mirabella thought to herself.

She threaded her way round the manor house, then stepped onto a path that would lead (if memory served correctly) directly to the tinkling marble fountain set in the middle of her godmama's gardens. The fountain had been erected in the center of a rich garden, in which visitors could sit upon benches and enjoy a grand view of every path leading inward.

Mirabella hurried down stone walkways flanked by blooming verbena, trailing vines, and leafy trees. Bees buzzed. Birds trilled. Finally, there came the not-so-distant sound of water splashing into the Grecian fountain ahead.

Mirabella stopped as she espied a woman who surely must be the Duchess of Ravenscar, resplendent in a morning gown of pink muslin, wringing her hands and looking both forlorn and fit to be tied as she paced back and forth in front of the marble fountain. The woman presented a comely picture, with her dark hair swept up into one fat ringlet coiling down her neck. Though plump, the duchess carried her weight well. Her skin was flawless, but flushed, and her eyes were the color of forest moss. She was crying quietly, if somewhat dramatically. Her round shoulders shuddered with each deep, quivering breath she drew.

Mirabella momentarily felt a beast for what she was about to do. How cruel to deceive the woman. She should just present herself and give the duchess the news that her precious Max was gone, never to return. But what would happen when the duchess dissolved into a fit of the vapors? According to Annie, the duchess would be a viper looking for blood—once she was finished with her fainting spells, of course. She would cause a ruckus in Aunt Nellie's household, mayhap even demand that Mirabella's precious Sasha be shot on sight.

That was something Mirabella would not abide. Sasha was too sweet, too dear, to be cut down in the prime of life! Mirabella had no choice but to attempt to pass off the counterfeit Max to the duchess.

Sending up a quick prayer for help—and gathering her courage—Mirabella called out a greeting. "Excuse me, your grace, but I believe I have found your spaniel."

The duchess took one look at Mirabella holding the pup in her arms and screeched in delight. "You have found my darling Max!"

"Er, yes," said Mirabella, choking on the lie. She set the pup on the ground and urged him toward the duchess. "Here is Max . . . right as rain, as you can see. Your pup merely got lost, I think."

"Well, of course he was lost," said the duchess. "Max would never purposely run away!" She captured the dog in a tight grip, then straightened, hugging the poor animal to her generous bosom. "Dear Max! How Mummy has missed you!" She ruffled the dog's silky ears, making the pup squeeze its eyes tight at her ardent caresses. The duchess beamed brightly as she glanced over at Mirabella. "How kind of you, my dear, to return my Max to me! We haven't met before, have we? Are you new to Stormhaven? You must be! Regina, the Duchess of Ravenscar, never forgets a name, or a face . . . and *your* face, my dear, I would remember. You are so pretty! Tell me, what is your name?"

"Mirabella Darlington. I am—"

"You are none other than Penelope's goddaughter, of course!" interrupted the duchess. "I have heard ever so much about you, my dear. Your wonderful godmama sings your praises daily, as well as those of your cousins, Miss Meredith and Miss Marcie. One would think you three Darlington cousins were heavenly angels come to grace the earth! Nellie adores all of you!"

Mirabella smiled, murmured her thanks, and felt a perfect devil. How could she even think to trick the duchess by delivering a false Max? It just wasn't right. The duchess should know the truth ... but, of course, to tell the truth would place Sasha in danger. *Oh, bother,* thought Mirabella, feeling caught between a rock and a hard place. *What to do?*

She was just about to return Max's diamond-studded collar to her grace when a tiny sparrow came spiraling down from a tree. It perched momentarily atop the Grecian fountain, warbling a hearty tune, then ruffled its wings and darted down to the feet of the duchess, where it pecked nervously at the ground. The pup, its attention on the bird, wriggled frantically against the duchess's hold. It struggled so mightily that her grace was forced to hold the pup aloft ...

The duchess stared at the creature as though it had sprouted two heads. She let out a shrill scream, looking for all the world as though she would faint dead away.

"Oooohhh, my precious Max, but you have been disfigured most horribly!" she screeched.

Mirabella jumped in surprise. And then realization dawned. *The counterfeit Max should have been a he, and not a she!*

" ... maligned most foully!" the appalled duchess screamed. "My sweet, poor Max has been c-castrated! Who could be so cruel as to do such a thing?"

Mirabella wished the earth would open up and swallow her whole. Why, oh why, hadn't she inquired as to the sex of the spaniel?

Mirabella watched as the counterfeit Max, rambunctious as always, jumped out of her grace's hold and darted off after the sparrow that had taken flight with the duchess's shriek of terror.

The Duchess of Ravenscar stumbled back a step, plopping her generous girth onto a marble bench. She quickly reached for the smelling salts she wore looped about her neck. "Oh, horror of all horrors!" she moaned.

Mirabella rushed forward. "There must be some mistake, your grace. I—I must have come across the wrong dog. Yes, that is it. I—I simply delivered the wrong pup to you!"

But her grace wasn't listening—in fact, she was beginning to breathe erratically. In another moment, Mirabella feared the woman would be lying prone on the ground and she herself would be left to the task of reviving a blue-lipped duchess!

At that very moment a low, masculine voice sounded behind Mirabella. "So, we meet again."

She whirled about, her heart giving a kick as she came face-to-face with the obsidian-eyed gentlemen who had so boldly kissed her at the fair. *"You!"* she gasped. "How dare you follow me? I ask you to leave, sir. Can you not see that I am in the midst of—"

"Chaos?" he finished for her, and rather arrogantly at that, thought Mirabella. "You seem to be forever in the midst of a storm, fair lady. Perhaps someone *should* follow you—if only to save you from the trouble you continually fall into."

Mirabella was about to deliver a scathing setdown, but he did not give her the chance. He looked past her to the duchess, who had progressed from wheezing to openly weeping. "I believe I have just the thing to cure her grace's blue-devils," he said, nodding at something he was carrying in his arms.

Only then did Mirabella manage to pull her gaze from the gentleman's aristocratic, very masculine features and take note of the cane he held in one hand—and the snoozing pup in the other. 'Twasn't just any ordinary pup, but a King Charles spaniel that, Mirabella was certain, was a *he*, not a *she*.

"Max's double, I presume?" she said hotly, beneath her breath.

The man grinned. "One can only hope." He reached for the collar Mirabella held in her hands and affixed it to the pup. "Now, if you'll excuse me? As you can see, I am on a mission," he added, purposely repeating the words she'd said at the fair.

Mirabella simmered as the man moved past her, heading for her grace, who was simultaneously waving smelling salts beneath her nose and mopping at her eyes with her kerchief.

"Your grace, do dry your eyes. I bring you Max. Will you take a look, my lady? I dare swear there are numerous King Charles spaniels cavorting about the Cotswolds"—here he sent a quick glance at Mirabella—"and I would be most upset if I brought you the wrong pup."

The duchess dabbed at her eyes, drew in a shaky breath, and then made a brave attempt to inspect the pup he held before her. "Oh!" she said, daring to look at the nether regions of the dog's plump belly, "I do believe you *have* found my precious Max! What a savior you are! What a true gallant!" The duchess gathered the new pup to her breast, raining kisses on its nose, head, and ears. "How I have missed my darling Max! I shall be forever in your debt, my good man!"

Mirabella watched as he bowed deeply and gave her grace a melting smile. What a preening cock of the walk he was! Mirabella thought. She knew for a fact he was nothing more than a cad, loose fish, a—a skirter! His stolen kiss in the Gypsy tent had told her that much! How dare he play the noble knight? But play the part he did, and very handsomely at that! He helped guide her grace to her feet, and even patted the docile pup on the head.

The Duchess of Ravenscar beamed at him. With a wave to Mirabella, and several more heartfelt thanks to the gentleman, her grace happily wandered into the gardens, cooing over her "precious little Max."

"I do believe the duchess will be pleased with her new dog. I made great pains to find a suitably docile pup. By the by," said the man, turning toward Mirabella, "where is the pup you chose?"

"Gone," she replied, hating to admit it. "He, er, she ... ran off ... a-after a bird, I fear." Was that amusement she perceived shimmering in the depths of his jet-black eyes? She was certain it was. "You are enjoying this, aren't you?" she snapped, unable to stop herself. "It amuses you that the pup I delivered to her grace was a woeful substitution for Max, while yours proved to be the perfect match."

A ghost of a grin played at the corners of his mouth. "What amuses me is the fact that the pup you purchased seems every bit the free spirit you appear to be. It isn't every day I encounter a lady searching tents at a fair, being proposed to by a Gypsy, and later surrounded by piglets. Tell me, are all your mornings as eventful as this one?"

Mirabella instantly deduced the gentleman was not the sort who would suffer any disturbance in his life. No doubt he was a stickler for convention, demanding precision and orderliness at all costs. Mirabella, however, was the exact opposite, and she took great delight in telling him so.

"As a matter of fact, sir," she said, "this morning has been nothing much out of the ordinary for me."

"I shudder to think what mayhem might transpire come evening," he murmured.

If only he knew! thought Mirabella, recalling her tiger on the loose, and the possible phantom haunting her godmama's grounds.

"Perhaps you *do* have need of a knight to watch over you," he added.

His words recalled to mind that moment in the tent when he'd so boldly kissed her. Something inside Mirabella's chest gave a lurch. She felt her cheeks pinken as he gazed at her. She didn't even know his name, yet he made her feel as though he could read her innermost thoughts. Was he, too, thinking of that kiss? Forcing herself not to melt beneath his heated stare, Mirabella lifted her chin and strove for composure.

"On the contrary, sir, I am quite capable of seeing to my own welfare. As for what mayhem I might encounter this evening, you needn't concern yourself. I doubt I shall see you again." With that, she gave him a crisp nod and headed out of the garden.

5

Mirabella hurried toward the house, her insides roiling with unsettled emotions. The man had an uncanny ability to unnerve her, and she did not like it. She only prayed he wasn't one of her godmama's guests, for if she ever laid eyes on him again it would be a moment too soon! Perhaps he'd purchased the neighboring James estate that had been for sale when Mirabella had last visited Stormhaven. She sincerely hoped that was the case and that he wasn't—God help her—inhabiting one of Aunt Nellie's many guest rooms.

Mirabella moved quickly across the stone terrace and popped open the French doors, so completely lost in thought that she nearly ran smack-dab into her godmama, who appeared to be on her way out.

"Aunt Nellie!" she said, coming to an abrupt halt.

"Ah, Bella, here you are!" exclaimed Penelope. "I have been anxiously awaiting your return, my dear!" She wasted no time in gathering Mirabella into a generous hug. She placed loving kisses on each of Mirabella's cheeks, and then held her at arm's length, enjoying a moment of pure pleasure in just gazing at her. "Ah, you are even more breathtakingly beautiful than I remember. And just look at your costume—how marvelous! I simply *adore* the outfit, my dear! I cannot tell you how I have missed your colorful company these many months!"

"And I have missed you, Auntie," Mirabella said, her heart warming at the sight of her godmama. She smiled broadly, barely noticing the fact that her godmama was dressed in harem pants, a garish vest, and a cutaway coat that did wonders for her smart figure.

"Shame on you, Bella, for not seeking me out the moment you arrived! But I shan't scold you overly much, for Annie told me you had a passion to visit one of the fairs in Stow. I'm so glad to hear you haven't outgrown your love of the fairs! Tell me, did you enjoy your outing?"

Mirabella hesitated, recalling the kiss the gentleman had stolen and later his strong and warm embrace as he'd guided her away from the piglets. "Let me just say that it was, er, eventful," she said. She wasn't of a mind to discuss the morning's events with Aunt Nellie. In fact, she wished to forget them (and the man) entirely. "You are looking splendid, Auntie," she said instead.

Penelope beamed. "And I am feeling splendid, now that you are here. We have thirteen months of catching up to do! You must tell me *all* about your exciting travels, my dear. But first, you must go upstairs and rest, as I have something very special planned for this evening."

"Special?" asked Mirabella, not missing the twinkle in her godmama's eyes. "Do not say that you are staging one of your famous séances tonight, Aunt Nellie!" she said, fearing the answer. The last time she'd joined one of her godmama's "calling forth of the spirits," the aged but spritely Countess of Coventry had summoned her dead husband, Jasper, and roundly cursed him for leaving her to deal with an illegitimate son, who had tried—but failed—to bribe a fortune from her. Aunt Nellie's guests had been scandalized, Penelope had been amused, and the countess, always one to brew a tempest in a teapot, had thoroughly enjoyed shocking everyone.

"No, no," assured Penelope. "My next séance will not take place until the end of the week. 'Tis a simple party I've planned for tonight, with but thirty or forty guests in attendance."

"*Only* thirty or forty?" teased Mirabella.

" 'Tis not so many, considering the size of Stormhaven. And there'll be dancing—leastways I *hope* there will be dancing. I've had a dueced difficult time scaring up a group of suitable musicians. I need not tell you what a challenge it has been to find competent musicians in the country at such short notice!"

"I can well imagine," said Mirabella, hiding a grin. "But truly, Auntie, you needn't go to such a fuss. I'll be happy enough to spend my evening alone with you. In truth, I would much prefer your company to that of a crush of people."

"Now, Bella, you must have a proper homecoming. I insist! I wish to show you off to my houseguests and reunite you with our neighbors. Lord knows I've bent their ears often enough, singing your praises. Everyone is anxious to meet you or become reacquainted with you."

Though Mirabella had been looking forward to a quiet evening, she found she could deny her godmama nothing. "A party would be marvelous," she said with a soft smile.

Penelope squeezed Mirabella's hands. "I was hoping you would say that, my dear! Now, do forgive me, but I must rush off. I have to deliver a personal invitation to Lord Blackwood, who is residing in the guest house. I am hoping he'll join us tonight. He's been a recluse of late, keeping to himself and venturing out only to make use of my spa."

"Oh?" asked Mirabella, her interest piqued. "And why is that?"

"It's a long story, involving a deceitful lady and a bullet taken in his thigh at Waterloo. Lord Blackwood has come to Stormhaven to heal his wound—and, I pray, his heart. There are those who say he has become a brooding, stuffy sort."

"But you know better," guessed Mirabella.

"Indeed I do," replied Penelope. "Christian is a man who has had his heart cleaved in two. Given time, he will come round, I am certain. I think you will like him, Bella. He is well-read, has a thirst for knowledge, and enjoys sketching and solitude—just as you do."

Mirabella's gaze narrowed. "Auntie," she said, "you wouldn't be considering any matchmaking, I pray."

"Heavens, no! 'Twould be a gross waste of time, I vow. You are, and ever have been, the Unmatchable Miss Mirabella."

Mirabella wrinkled her nose. "How I detest that silly title. I am hardly 'unmatchable,' Aunt Nellie. It is just that I have yet to encounter a man with whom I could envision spending the rest of my days."

But even as she said the words, Mirabella's mind conjured up an image of the handsome gentleman who had so ridiculously entangled himself with a dancing bear and then calmed a flighty duchess.

Why the deuce she should think of him now—or ever again—was beyond Mirabella. Imagine, being so preoccupied with a man, and one she'd barely met!

The sound of Penelope's voice jolted Mirabella's thoughts back to the present.

"I assure you I am not a matchmaking terror," said her godmama. "I only thought you and

Christian would find common ground. As I've said, he is a contemplative fellow, and remains one of my truest friends. His dear departed mother and I were bosom bows. I've known Christian since his nursery days. But I am worried about the turn he's taken in life. He keeps to himself too much of late, and I fear he is a bit too strapped by convention. To those who do not know him he can appear a cold sort. But there beats a heart of pure gold in his chest."

"You truly do adore him, don't you, Aunt Nellie?" said Mirabella.

"I do," Penelope answered. "He is like the son I never had. You will adore him as well, Bella, for like you he has a quick mind. And he is ever so handsome! His eyes are the color of midnight, and he sports a comely wave of hair that tumbles down his forehead."

Mirabella started. Her godmama's description matched that of the obsidian-eyed gentleman who'd plagued her. She was suddenly certain the two were one and the same. *Oh, bother!*

Penelope, unaware of her goddaughter's thoughts, gave a quick kiss to Mirabella's forehead, and told her to go upstairs and rest, and leave all the details of the party to her.

Mirabella, watching Penelope depart, gazed miserably after her. She had had her misgivings about a welcome-home party; now she absolutely dreaded it!

Blackwood had watched as the outrageously dressed miss had exited the gardens, heading toward Penelope's house. Suddenly enlightenment had dawned. He should have guessed from the start that the lady, with her queer garb and three earrings in each ear, was a houseguest of the ever-surprising Penelope Barrington. It was highly

The Unmatchable Miss Mirabella 57

likely that the two of them *would* meet again, much to the lady's consternation, no doubt—and mayhap even his own.

Though Blackwood considered self-reliance a virtue (and the lady certainly had *that*), he'd now begun to think her a tad too original for her own good. She was fortunate she hadn't been abducted by that Gypsy at the fair. What was she thinking to gad about the countryside on her own? She obviously needed a stern hand in her life, as she herself had said that the morning's events were "nothing much out of the ordinary." *Nothing much out of the ordinary?* Zounds, what topsy-turvy life did she live? And as for the way in which she'd trembled when he'd stolen a kiss from her earlier, she would land herself in trouble if she reacted to every man she met that way!

Blackwood frowned, appalled to reconsider his own roguish behavior with the miss in the Gypsy tent. The kiss had been very much against the grain of his usual impeccable conduct. He'd kissed her only as a ploy to see the Gypsy gone. Nothing more. And yet, the memory of his mouth on hers lingered; he could still taste her sweetness, recall her provocative scent.

Blackwood turned away from the fountain and made his way to the opposite end of the garden, to a stone path that led to the guest house. It was a long walk to the small but airy cottage situated high atop the knoll behind Stormhaven—long enough for him to think about the miss at some length.

Her independent ways reminded him of his brother Matthew, who had been two years his senior and had attained the Blackwood title following their father's death. Her smile, dash it all, brought to mind Lady Diana, the woman he'd once thought to marry ... Diana of the violet eyes, whose smile flashed brighter than the sun, and whose final deceit had left him reeling. While Blackwood had battled the French at Waterloo, Matthew and Diana had been busy with their own private lives. They'd died in each other's arms, the focus of one of the most talked-about scandals among the *ton*. Blackwood had returned to England an injured war hero, only to bury his brother and his fiancée the very same week he ascended to his title. Seclusion within Penelope's guest house had brought a measure of comfort and much-needed time away from home, where there were too many memories of Matthew and Diana. Blackwood thought he'd exorcised the ghost of the ever-flirtatious Diana. Now, however, he wasn't so certain. The woman he'd kissed in the tent reminded him too much of her; she, too, had been reckless, a great beauty who did not realize the power of her charm. Blackwood's thoughts turned dark. He was glad when the cottage came into view.

It was a quaint structure, set against a backdrop of towering elms, and built of honey-colored stone with circular windows facing south. Bright wildflowers grew in profusion along its sides. Reaching the front entrance, Blackwood lifted the latch, stepped inside the handsomely furnished foyer, then pushed the portal shut behind him with the tip of his cane. It goaded him no small amount that he had need of a cane at all. His only balm was in knowing that the carrying of a fine cane was all the rage, considered a sign of breeding and taste.

Leaving the walking stick in the hall beneath the polished hat rack, he entered the adjoining sitting room and poured himself a stiff glass of brandy. The liquid burned a path down his throat, warming him. He took great pleasure in the fact that the steep jaunt up the knoll hadn't overly irritated his injured thigh. His wound was healing—if only his heart could mend as well.

Blackwood sipped at the brandy, recalling that moment in the garden when he'd come upon the queerly outfitted miss. She had thought he'd been following her (what a ridiculous notion!), and though she'd obviously been unnerved by the possibility, she had brazenly ordered him to leave.

Pity she found herself in one scandal broth after another. The Gypsy who'd proposed to her had seemed to Blackwood a tad too intent. No doubt the fellow would contrive another meeting with her—and would doubtless challenge Blackwood to a duel should they ever cross paths again.

He set down his glass of brandy, glanced up at the gleaming, fine Florentine rapiers affixed over the mantel, and knew a strong urge to take one of the rapiers in his hand. He did just that, testing the strength of the weapon against his boot, and wondering, should he be pressed, if he would actually duel for the lady.

He went through the motions of executing a perfect *quarte*. His blade caught the sunlight streaming through the windows and glinted brightly. He parried effortlessly, imagining his foe, then initiated an unrelenting attack to the high lines of that opponent. It felt good, pushing his thigh muscle to the ultimate test. He parried, thrust, riposted with ease. With a firmly flicking wrist, he cut a ribbon of silver through the air, his blade making clean hissing sounds. He hadn't lost his touch, he thought, pleased.

There came a whisper of motion from the doorway behind him. He swung round, the rapier held firm in his fist.

"Christian!" said Penelope Barrington. She smiled round the mouthpiece of her pipe, the bowl and stem of which were carved into a decadent scene of human and animal forms, limbs entwined. "You are fencing again!" she said, her voice an awed whisper.

"Was," he corrected. He lowered the rapier.

"You needn't stop on my account."

"I'm not. I am finished for the day."

"Are you? Hmmm, I wonder." Penelope leaned against the doorjamb, fixing him with an ageless gaze that Blackwood found far too probing. "Looks to me as though you've just begun."

Blackwood cocked one dark brow at her. "Always the critic, eh? I thought my motions were very smooth." He adored Penelope Barrington. How could he not? She'd been the truest of friends, offering him her guest house and some much-needed solitude. Blackwood rested the tip of his sword against his boot and half-smiled. "Don't you ever knock, Nellie?" he asked.

"Lord, no," she replied. "It would be an utter waste of time, Christian. At the moment, your servants are all gathered round my cook's chopping block. She is bent on teaching them the precise way of roasting kid."

"I suspect my servants are gathered in your kitchens only to avoid me."

"Well, if that's the case, I can't say as I blame them. You have been odious of late, Christian, barking at your servants and hibernating from your friends."

"I do not deny it."

"Of course you don't. Nor do you make any apologies. That's what I like most about you. You are what you are, and if the world doesn't like it, then it can go to the devil for all you care. But I know for a fact that your bark is worse than your bite. I happened across the duchess on my way up here. She told me you returned her Max to her.

Thank you, Christian. I knew I could count on you."

Blackwood nodded. "You are most welcome. Anything for you, dear Nellie."

Penelope moved into the room. He noticed that she wore, of all things, harem pants, slippers with tiny gold tassels, and a diaphanous blouse that, without the small vest embroidered with fire-breathing dragons and two-headed serpents, would have shown to shocking advantage all of her expansive bosom. Atop this outlandish costume she sported a man's cutaway coat made of crushed blue velvet, cut close so as to accentuate her fine figure. A white turban covered her blonde hair, and in the center of the turban winked a blue diamond as big as a walnut. She wore bangles, curled like snakes, on both wrists, and each of her fingers sparkled with the glint of gems.

Blackwood eyed her with interest, as he always did. He'd never met—nor would he ever meet, he hazarded—a woman as compelling and entertaining as Penelope Barrington. Save, perhaps, for the miss at the fair.

She met his gaze head-on, smiling that mystical smile that had led countless men to distraction and several to the altar.

"My dear Christian," she said, "toss me that other rapier, will you?"

"Surely you jest, Penelope."

"Not at all," she replied. "I haven't fenced in an age, I vow. Will you take the weapon down for me, or shall I be forced to pluck it from the wall myself?"

"I will do the deed, Nellie," he said, grinning at her outlandish ways, "but do not think I will remove the point guards." He took the weapon down and tossed it to her.

Penelope easily caught the hilt and took a moment to admire the sword's fine craftsmanship. "Did I ever tell you the story of my ever-so-great-grandfather who once owned these swords? He was a Calvinist heretic who tried to convert sixteenth-century folks to his own beliefs. He died at the blade of one of these very swords. 'Twas a messy affair, to be sure. My ancestors thought him a black sheep. I, however, prefer to think of him as being colorful and brave. *En garde*, Christian," she added suddenly, lifting the sword.

"Penelope! Please," Blackwood said. "I would hate to have to best you."

"Ah, arrogant as always, eh?" she said. "You flatter yourself! I could cut you down with but one flick of my wrist."

"A gentleman does not fence with a lady."

"You are, and ever have been, too strapped by the rules of genteel Society, my dear Christian. Do take care, lest people think you've become a stuffed shirt."

At that, Blackwood indulged her. He flexed his sword.

Penelope, grinning, saluted him formally, then took several steps back. The match began. Penelope opened aggressively, surprising Blackwood. He parried, their blades clashing, sparking at the contact. They circled each other, Penelope still biting down on the stem of her ridiculous pipe, and Blackwood wondering what the devil she was about. It was then that she advanced. He met the attack with a smooth parry and riposte, yet every counterriposte was coolly repelled.

"You are very good," he said.

"Of course I am. Do not forget that it was I who introduced you to the fine art of fencing, dear Christian."

"I haven't forgotten," he said, feinting to the right. She moved after him with the precise skill of a master. "Good God, Penelope! What is your purpose?"

Her rich laughter filled the room as she backed him against the wall near the hearth. "I have come to invite you to a party, my dear Christian."

"Faith!" he breathed. "Could you not send an invitation, like normal folk?"

"And run the risk of having you deny me? Perish the thought, my dear!" She lowered the rapier, smiling as she did so. "I have planned a party for my goddaughter. I expect you to be there."

"Oh?" Blackwood said.

She nodded. "You must make an appearance, as I have invited an odd number of ladies and need but one more male to even out my guest list."

"Rubbish. Tell me true, Penelope."

She sighed deeply. "Oh, very well," she admitted. "I thought you might enjoy meeting my goddaughter. I do believe she is just your cup of tea, Christian. She abhors crowds, harbors an inquisitive mind, is vastly independent, and she loves to sketch—just as you do."

"And is she anything like her singular godmama?" Blackwood asked, smiling as he relieved Penelope of her sword.

"But of course! She even has my flair for fashion."

Blackwood's grin deepened as he turned to replace the swords on the wall above the mantelpiece. "Tell me more," he said.

"Her father died little more than a year ago. Left her an heiress. He was a banker, one of the Darlington Three. Went into business with his two brothers and the three of them made a fortune in their myriad investments. Her mother died when she was but a girl and her papa, forever a restless sort, itched to scour the world, learn its secrets and all. He took Bella with him, of course, for she was ever the apple of his eye, and she grew up amid faraway places. She speaks more languages than I have fingers. Hers is a very sweet soul. You must meet her, Christian."

"Bella, is it?"

"Mirabella Lavinia Darlington, to be exact, but she is known about Town as the Unmatchable Miss Mirabella. I fear bucks are forever falling at her feet. Alas, she is not in the least interested. You see, her father—and even I myself—encouraged her from the cradle to be a free and independent spirit. I dare swear it will take an enlightened fellow to turn her thoughts to marriage. In the meantime, however, I fear she is destined to be forever plagued by gentlemen who fall instantly in love with her."

Blackwood knew then without a doubt that Miss Mirabella Lavinia Darlington and the miss he'd kissed at the fair were one and the same. He considered telling Penelope he had already met her goddaughter but decided against it. He hadn't made the best impression where Miss Darlington was concerned. Too, she had made it vividly clear that she wanted nothing more to do with him. Doubtless she had decided to put the incident at the fair behind her. He would do the same.

"So," said Penelope, cutting into Blackwood's thoughts, "may I count on you to join us this evening, Christian? I should be fair and warn you, though, that Lord Montague Warwick will be present. He arrived yesterday."

"*Monty* is here?" Blackwood said, not at all pleased. The muscles of his jaw tightened. Warwick, a womanizer of the first degree, had relentlessly pursued Diana in the days before Blackwood had ridden off to battle—and Diana, blast her, had responded to his flirtations. "What the deuce are you thinking, entertaining that cad, Nellie?"

"Now, Christian," Penelope soothed, "Lord Monty is not the perfect devil you think him. He does have his faults, I admit—"

"He's a scoundrel! You know as well as I do that he pursues a lady only after he's considered the size of her purse. He's gambling away his inheritance, has siphoned funds from his many married mistresses, and still he plays the Marriage Mart as though he has every right to do so."

"Yes, I know," said Penelope, "but he does add spice to a gathering, does he not? Besides, my dear Christian, he presented himself on my doorstep and I could hardly turn him away!"

"Whyever not? I've never known you to mince words, Nellie."

"True," she admitted. "But I've taken it upon myself to help alleviate the poor living conditions of factory workers in the north. It behooves my cause to woo members of Parliament—and you and I both know Lord Monty will soon be taking his seat there. Despite his faults, he remains well connected."

"He hardly deserves a seat in Parliament," muttered Blackwood.

"I agree, but that is the way of it and I do not intend to insult him ... which brings me to the other reason I came here today. Lord Monty showed great interest in my goddaughter when he last saw her, before she departed for Bengal. Given that Bella has come into her inheritance, I believe Lord Monty's pursuit of her will intensify. Now, it isn't that I don't think Bella can manage him, for I do. She is not one to be fooled, foiled, or even fussed over. But I am concerned about how Lord Monty will react when she gives him a set-down. To support my own cause, I don't want Monty feeling alienated. As for Bella, I don't want her to have to endure Monty's deceitful flirtations. I was hoping, Christian, that you would be present this evening to help keep the two of them apart."

"Say no more," he replied, thinking of Bella's forthright ways, her shattering beauty—and, of course, that mystical, wondrous *something* about her that had prompted a Gypsy to go down on bended knee and propose, that *something* that had caused Blackwood himself to kiss her. "I shall attend your party, Nellie," he assured her. "And I will, I promise you, safeguard your goddaughter from Monty's wiles."

"Thank you," said Penelope. "Once again, I knew I could count on you." She leaned forward, gave him a quick kiss on the cheek, then made ready to leave.

Blackwood escorted her to the door. When he was once again alone, his mind filled with thoughts of Miss Darlington and the womanizing Warwick. In Warwick's view, the young and beautiful and rich Bella would seem the perfect bloom to pluck.

Blackwood balked at the very notion. He knew only too well the vile, deceitful ways of Lord Monty, had seen the rake in action far too many times, and he had, damn it all, endured the pain of watching Lady Diana be swayed by Monty's false words of love. He would not suffer the same again. Nor would he allow Monty to blacken the free-spirited Mirabella Darlington. He would play her knight this evening, and for as often as needed thereafter. Whether she liked it or not, he would be her bodyguard.

Problem was, Blackwood knew she wouldn't like it. Not one bit.

6

Mirabella hastened upstairs, as her godmama had suggested, but did not immediately rest. Instead, she summoned Haluk and Annie.

Haluk, always ready to do her bidding, bowed. Trussed up in a too-tight coat, he looked like a woeful footman. Annie, standing beside him, beamed, clearly thinking she'd done a famous job of securing Haluk a proper outfit.

"Are you pleased, Miss Bella?" she asked.

Mirabella could only nod. Obviously, both the maid and Haluk were happy with his ill-fitting attire. She decided not to point out that the Turk's coat was much too small or that his boots were obviously pinching his large feet. Instead, she suggested that Haluk and Annie venture out to find Sasha and the female spaniel that had scurried away; Haluk should scout for Sasha and Annie should try to find the wayward pup. The pair was only too eager to go off together. Mirabella was glad to see that Haluk had made a new friend. Perhaps, instead of returning to his homeland, he would make a niche for himself at Stormhaven.

Before leaving, Annie assured Mirabella that she'd located her missing trunks and had taken the initiative in choosing a gown for her to wear to the party.

"Thank you, Annie," said Mirabella, glad to have one less thing to worry about.

Once they were gone, she kicked off her slippers

and sat down on the edge of the large, four-poster bed. It felt heavenly to rest her weary body; her journey home and the eventful visit to the fair had overtaxed her emotions. She lay down, thinking only to rest her eyes for a moment or two. She fully intended to go downstairs and help oversee preparations for the party, but before she knew it, she was fast asleep.

Mirabella slept until after the sun set. She came awake with a start, wondering for a moment where she was. She took one look at the many traveling trunks shadowing the room and memory returned to her. She was now at Stormhaven, with her godmama. She was *home*.

She stretched languidly. Through the open windows she could hear the haunting cries of Penelope's ornamental peafowl, which inhabited the northern reaches of the gardens, as well as the soft splashing of the fountain, the squabbling of busy sparrows, and the far-off sound of Aunt Nellie's Cotswold sheep bleating in the pastures.

For a moment, Mirabella could almost imagine her father's robust voice, calling her to come join him for an evening's stroll. She hastened to the window seat, leaned out—as she used to do when she was a child—and peered down into the gardens now lit with the flickering light of a hundred Chinese lanterns that had been strung about. *Papa, wait for me!* she nearly called out, forgetting for a moment that he wasn't in the gardens, waiting for her as he used to do.

Mirabella sank back down onto the window seat, feeling sad as the remembered sound of her father's voice echoed in her mind, in her heart. She had come to Stormhaven to heal her soul, yet her memories of this place had the power to make her weep.

Dear Papa, she thought, *how I miss you*. She

brushed the wetness from her eyes, took a deep breath, and forced herself to remember that her father would not wish for her to be such a watering pot her first night home. He would want her to enjoy Aunt Nellie's party, would insist that she dance until dawn, be gay and carefree, and ever and always be true to the lively spirit he'd nurtured within her. So thinking, Mirabella turned away from the window and set her thoughts to the party to come.

She pulled the rope bell, summoning Annie to help her dress. After waiting for fifteen minutes, Mirabella deduced the maid was still combing the grounds for the runaway spaniel. After another pull of the bell, a flustered young Meg came to do Mirabella's bidding.

"I *am* sorry, Miss Darlington!" apologized the brown-haired, sweet-looking Meg. She bobbed a quick curtsy. "Annie asked me to see to your toilette, but I did not think I would be so long in arranging the flowers in the ballroom downstairs, and then one of the kitchen maids got sick and I had to help carve the roast kid!"

"No need to worry yourself," said Mirabella, hoping to soothe the girl's agitated state. She could well imagine the amount of work that was going into her godmama's party. "As long as I have hot water for my bath, I can attend to my own toilette," she added.

Meg looked relieved. "Oh, there be hot water for you, Miss Darlington. That I did see to!"

Meg shyly motioned Mirabella to the adjoining chamber where there was a tub filled with scented water. For Mirabella, a long and leisurely bath was like manna from heaven. An hour later, Meg proved to be a wizard with comb and brush. At long last, Mirabella was ready to don the gown Annie had chosen ... too bad for her that Annie had opened the first trunk available—one Mirabella had packed in the wilds of Rangoon, when she'd been in a most free-spirited mood. She lifted up a sheath of white moire silk that was exceedingly low-cut. It was to be worn with dampened petticoats lest the smooth lines of the gown be ruined.

Mirabella frowned, considered having another, more appropriate gown pressed, but knew there was no time. Oh, bother! But what was done could not be undone without a great fuss, and so Mirabella donned the white silk gown and dampened petticoats.

Annie had also dug deep into the trunk to procure what she'd deemed suitable gems to complement the outfit. Mirabella now sported dangling Byzantine earrings, several hammered gold bracelets, and a pretty star ornament affixed to her carefully knotted hair. The result was stunning, Mirabella had to admit. She chose delicate slippers and a lightweight Kashmir shawl to complete her ensemble.

It was a little early to go down to the party, but the room was stuffy and Mirabella decided to sit by the fountain in the gardens before greeting Penelope's guests. As she emerged from the house, she took a deep breath of cool Cotswold air. The gardens teemed with sounds and scents. Evening birds ruffled their wings, singing and darting about. The heady smell of roses hung on the breeze.

Mirabella moved to the marble parapet surrounding the fountain's pool. She perched there, her mind caught up in remembering her father, of thinking of the night to come, and dreading the moment when she would formally meet Lord Blackwood. She wished her father were alive now. Doubtless he would have an opinion of how she could handle the unnerving Lord Blackwood! Her thoughts were broken when a man stepped into the clearing.

"Miss Bella? Good God, is it truly you? What a vision you are! A lovely angel come to earth!"

Mirabella winced at the sound of Lord Montague Warwick's voice. She watched as he moved closer to her. He wore a tall black hat atop his curly brown hair, a charcoal coat, tight-fitting white kerseymere breeches, and a gleaming diamond stickpin in the folds of his neckcloth.

"Hullo, Lord Warwick," Mirabella said, wishing the rake were anywhere but Stormhaven. "I didn't know you'd come to visit my godmama."

Warwick stepped beneath the Chinese lanterns burning bright near the fountain. The light caught and sparkled in his cunning eyes. "I came only to see your beauteous countenance once again, my lovely Miss Bella."

Mirabella rose to her feet, forcing a smile. "Surely you exaggerate. I know for a fact that you take great delight in Aunt Nellie's séances, sir."

"Yes, but I came not for any calling of the spirits, but only in the hope of seeing you again. You remain as beautiful as I remember—nay, more so," he murmured, reaching to capture one of her gloved hands in both of his. He pressed a kiss to the back of it.

Mirabella forced herself not to curl her nose in distaste. She knew well what a womanizer Lord Montague Warwick was. He enjoyed courting any heiress, and left a trail of broken hearts behind him wherever he went.

"I believe you flatter me overly much, my lord," she replied.

"Never that, my lovely Miss Bella," he said. "Say you will save the supper dance for me. But if I may be wholly honest, I would be most honored if I could escort you inside and be the first man seen at your side tonight."

Mirabella wondered how she could get totally free of the man, not only for the supper dance but for the entire night! She was saved from answering when Annie came darting into the gardens just then.

"Miss Bella! Miss Bella! I done spied yer tiger—and that phantom, too!" she cried. She skidded to a dead halt, breathing mightily and remembering, belatedly, to drop a curtsy to both Mirabella and the finely dressed stranger. "Oh, la!" she breathed. "I didn't know you 'ad a visitor!" Lord Montague Warwick skewered Annie with a hearty frown.

Mirabella ignored the man's reaction and gave the girl a gentle smile. "Do tell, Annie," she said kindly. "Have you truly seen Sasha?"

"I—I think so," said Annie, "but it 'appened so fast I can't be certain. I do know I spied that 'andsome phantom! Wearin' black 'e was, and movin' at a fast clip down the path! Oh, do come, Miss Bella! I want you t' see the phantom!"

"Phantom?" Lord Warwick asked. "Do not tell me Annie has been dipping into Penelope's gin again," he murmured to Mirabella, as though Annie didn't exist and couldn't hear him.

Mirabella bristled. How rude of the man! She'd disliked him before, but now her dislike mounted tenfold.

Mirabella fixed her gaze on Annie, purposely ignoring his lordship. "Tell me, Annie, where did you espy this, uh, phantom?"

"Up there!" she said, shivering as she pointed toward the knoll slanting up from the house.

Mirabella decided once and for all to ferret out this "phantom." She moved toward the path with dogged determination.

"I can't let you go *alone!*" gasped Annie.

"Certainly not!" added Warwick.

Mirabella wished the both of them would leave her be, but did not argue when they trailed behind her. Long shadows encompassed them as Mirabella led the way up the twisting, winding path. A gibbous moon hung in the night sky above. Clouds smeared the dark sky, splintering the moon's rays, and the wind-rustled leaves in the trees played havoc with the eerie light.

"'Tis a night ripe for ghouls and phantoms!" whispered Annie, her voice quavering.

"Hush, Annie. You know there are no such things," said Mirabella.

There came a rustle of movement in front of them. Warwick, intending to act the gallant, forced the maid behind him, but failed to guide Mirabella behind him as well. She stood her ground, heart pounding. Out of the shadows stepped a tall, imposing figure, a weapon brandished in his right fist.

Annie let forth a bloodcurdling scream.

Lord Warwick cursed.

Mirabella frowned. "*You!*" she uttered, espying none other than the handsomely attired Lord Blackwood, sporting a fashionable rosewood cane.

At that moment Haluk, alarmed by Annie's scream, came charging through the twisting vines. Mirabella knew instantly what he was about. "Haluk, *no!*" she called.

Too late. The mighty Turk threw all his weight against the well-dressed gentleman, toppling him to the ground. There ensued a quick scuffle, during which Lord Blackwood successfully heaved Haluk's great weight off of him.

Mirabella rushed forward, capturing Haluk by one arm and pulling him away, fearing that Lord Blackwood would vent his rage on the man. "Say nothing," Mirabella warned Haluk. "You have just knocked over the Earl of Blackwood!"

Warwick astonished them all by hooting with laughter. "Christ's nails! It *is* you, Christian!"

"So it is," grunted Blackwood, righting himself. He glared at Mirabella and her entourage. "I should have guessed," he muttered. "Do not tell me—you have gone in search of yet another companion!"

"Th-the phantom," squeaked Annie, hiding behind Mirabella. "We thought you was 'e!"

"Why am I not surprised?" said Blackwood, not taking his eyes off Mirabella.

She felt her face flame. She could not help but notice his stormy gaze. "Forgive us, my lord. We-we did not intend to startle you."

"Startle me?" he exclaimed. "Your friend near knocked the breath out of me!"

"Haluk was only trying to protect me."

The Turk puffed up his chest with pride.

Blackwood frowned. "Yet another of your many followers, I presume," he murmured, his low voice meant only for Mirabella.

Her cheeks grew even hotter at his implication. "I trust you are not injured, my lord?" she asked, wanting only to end this absurd encounter.

"Only his pride is injured, I dare swear," said Lord Monty, not intending to be left out of the conversation. "Good God, Christian, fancy meeting you here. Word at White's is that you'd taken an extended holiday. Do not say you've been hiding yourself in Penelope's guest house yonder!"

"I was just on my way down to the main house to join Penelope's gathering." Blackwood turned his stormy gaze to Mirabella. "Miss Darlington?" he said, offering her his arm. "Would you do me the honor of allowing me to escort you back to the house?"

Mirabella had noted the telltale twitch of a muscle along Blackwood's strong jawline as he'd spoken to Warwick. She knew then that Blackwood did not care for the rakish Lord Montague Warwick. She decided against coolly reminding the Earl of Blackwood that they hadn't been properly introduced and that she wished to go nowhere with him. Of course, saying this would serve no purpose, and might even incite Lord Monty to speak up on her behalf. God only knew what might transpire then! Clearly, Lord Blackwood and Lord Monty were age-old enemies. Mirabella thought it best to simply accept Blackwood's invitation. The sooner she was clear of Blackwood's presence, the better!

Lord Monty, however, was not about to be forgotten. "You are too late, Christian," he said, taking great delight in baiting Blackwood. "I have already offered to escort Miss Bella inside ... and she has all but promised me her company this evening."

Mirabella's eyes widened, then narrowed as she met Lord Monty's smug gaze. "Sir," she began, intending to set him in his place, "I do not recall promising you any such thing—"

"Forget him." 'Twas Lord Blackwood's voice. He moved beside her and took her elbow in one hand, gripping it tightly. The look in his wintery eyes forbade denial. "Come along, Miss Darlington," he said. "You would do well to forget that insufferable cad."

Though he'd voiced Mirabella's thoughts exactly, she did not appreciate his presumption! "I am quite capable of taking my own self down the knoll," she told him.

"I am certain you are, my spirited lady. But I shall escort you nonetheless."

Mirabella was just about to pull ahead of him when Lord Monty said, "I demand you unhand the lady, Christian. Pray, allow Miss Bella to make her own decision."

"Demand and be damned," muttered Blackwood, not looking back. With that, he commenced to guide Mirabella down the steep and twisting path, leaving a fuming Lord Monty behind.

Mirabella gnashed her teeth, fighting to match Blackwood's long strides. "How dare you?" she said.

"I am a daring man."

"What you are is insufferably arrogant, thickheaded, and far too pompous for your own good!"

"And you, Miss Darlington, are forever landing yourself in one scandal broth after another. What the devil did that maid say you were searching for? A *phantom?* Faith!" he breathed. "What nonsense! You obviously need a strong hand in your life, my fair lady."

"Do quit addressing me in that ridiculous manner. I am not *your* anything, sir!" she replied. "Obviously my godmama has told you my name. I dare hope she has also informed you that I am not one to be heeled like some well-trained beast!"

He cocked one dark brow at her, not missing a beat in his fast-paced walk. "I never assumed you were, Miss Darlington. From what I've seen, you are beautiful, original, engaging, oft-times charming . . . and too damned spirited for your own good."

Mirabella opened her mouth, then shut it just as quickly, his words taking her by surprise. He found her charming? "I—I don't know whether to accept your words as a compliment or a cut, sir."

Blackwood's sensuous mouth twisted into a

half-smile. "Trust me when I say I wonder myself."

Mirabella fell silent then, hurrying along beside him. She took comfort in the knowledge that Haluk and Annie, trailed by Lord Monty, were following a short distance away. She did fear, however, that if Blackwood walked any faster, she would find herself tumbling head over heels down the snaking path.

"Zeus and Minerva!" she snapped. "Must you continue with such a hectic pace?"

"Yes," he snapped right back at her. "I wouldn't want you to be late for your godmama's party in your honor. Nor," he added, "would I want to miss being the first to sweep you onto the dance floor."

Mirabella considered giving him a stinging reply, of telling him she had no intention of dancing with him at all. But in the next instant, the man's pace slowed and he gave her a chance to catch her breath. He was not, after all, the heartless being he pretended to be. The thought warmed her, made her pulse and her stomach flutter. Too soon, they stepped onto a path that led to the lit gardens. And then, before Mirabella could calm her jittery nerves at the man's nearness, they came to the French doors leading inside the house.

Lord Blackwood swung the doors open, bowed slightly, then motioned her inside. "Your guests await you, Miss Darlington," he said, suddenly sounding like a true and gallant gentleman.

Mirabella moved past him, her shoulder brushing the hard muscle of his right arm. A jolt of electricity snapped through her at the contact. She chanced a glance at him. Their gazes met and held, his a deep, deep black, shadowed with mystery. She could not help but wonder what the coming night would hold for both of them.

7

Much to Mirabella's consternation, she found upon entering the house that the neighboring guests had all arrived and were already mingling with Penelope's houseguests in the front drawing room.

"Do not fret," said Lord Blackwood, apparently aware of her distress. "Since you do not wish to embarrass your godmama, who has doubtless been forced to make some excuse concerning your absence from the receiving line, what do you say we stage a late grand entrance for you, and play that it was your intention to do so all along?"

"But how?" asked Mirabella, hearing the babble of voices drifting from the front drawing room. She cursed herself for not joining Aunt Nellie sooner. Oh, what a mess she'd made of the party—and she had yet to make an entrance!

"Leave me to worry over the details," said Lord Blackwood. He motioned for Mirabella to take the servants' stairs to the second floor. "Head for the landing of the front staircase," he told her. "In the meantime, I shall alert Penelope to your arrival. Between the two of us, we shall ensure that your entrance is a smooth one."

Mirabella did as she was instructed, her heart pounding as she hurried up the servants' stairwell. Haluk and Annie thought to scurry after her, but Mirabella bade them continue their search for the runaway animals. The two did as she asked, leaving her alone to face the crowd below. She moved toward the landing of the wide and curving staircase, hoping Lord Blackwood proved true to his word. She would never forgive herself for being late to her own homecoming party!

Blackwood headed into the front drawing room, but not before Lord Monty came tearing after him.

"She isn't your type of woman," said Montague, dogging Blackwood's steps. "Do yourself a favor and forget her."

Blackwood halted, pausing long enough to give Lord Monty a healthy hint to begone. "You might have had your fun at the expense of my fiancée, Lady Diana, Monty, but I warn you now, I'll not suffer your presence near Miss Darlington."

Warwick laughed. "You sound threatened, Christian. Can I take this to mean you are interested in the comely Miss Bella? Lord, I never thought I'd see the day when anyone but the flirtatious Lady Diana could turn your head!"

"Perhaps," Blackwood said quietly, dangerously, "my tastes have changed." With that, he left Warwick.

He found Penelope surrounded by a circle of friends. She wore an outrageous creation of silks and bangles, with a blazing turquoise turban atop her blonde hair. "Christian!" she murmured as he politely guided her away from her friends. "Whatever is the matter?"

"Nothing," he replied. "I only wished to inform you that your goddaughter is waiting at the top of the stairs for you to introduce her."

"Heavens! I'd thought she'd decided to duck out of my gathering!"

"I fear she was detained in the gardens, chasing after a phantom."

"Ah," breathed Penelope, enlightenment dawning. "No doubt Annie led her on a wild-goose chase! Say no more, my dear Christian. What a blessing you are to bring Mirabella inside and to think of a way for her to make a proper entrance. Everyone will be forced to make a fuss over her, won't they?" she said, her blue eyes twinkling with mischief. "You must stand at the bottom of the stairs, Christian, and greet Bella as she makes her grand descent!"

"I doubt that she would approve," murmured Blackwood. "I haven't made the best of impressions where your goddaughter is concerned."

"Poppycock!" retorted Penelope. "You shall greet her at the bottom of the stairs, Christian, I insist! Only imagine the stir it will create—the reclusive Lord Blackwood awaiting the Unmatchable Miss Mirabella! I dare swear my guests will be quite tongue-tied, and will doubtless forgive the fact that Bella was not at the door to receive them."

Blackwood could not deny the ever-inventive Penelope Barrington. And so it was that he found himself leaving the drawing room to stand at the foot of the staircase. Penelope, meanwhile, thought to induce the musicians to play a grand tune as she instructed all of her guests to gather in the great hall. A flurry of activity took place.

Blackwood worried that Mirabella, not given to bothering herself with the strictures of Society, might have decided to forget the party entirely. But then he caught sight of her standing at the top of the stairs. His heart beat a wild rhythm. Lord, but she was beautiful in her clinging, shapely gown. Her fair skin glowed beneath the light of the chandelier. Her eyes flashed brightly, and her blonde hair seemed alive with the light of stars.

In her smoke-scratched voice, Penelope grandly announced her goddaughter. Mirabella took her cue, gliding effortlessly down the steps, her head held high.

Blackwood sucked in a deep breath. She was Beauty taken to great heights, her face too exquisite for words. He gave her a fashionable leg, knowing that the guests expected it of him. He was rewarded by the warm and tingling sensation of her hand on his arm.

"My lord," she murmured, playing her part perfectly.

Blackwood guided her off the last step. They stood side by side as a murmur of awe swept through the crowd. Only one person—Lord Monty—appeared not to be pleased. He glared at Blackwood, hatred in his brown gaze. Blackwood ignored the man.

The next hour flew by in a haze of heat and excitement. Blackwood enjoyed Mirabella's nearness too much. Since he'd escorted her into the room, she could hardly snub him, though she seemed to want to do so. He tucked her hand deep into the crook of his right arm, guiding her easily from one guest to the next.

He found himself liking the sound of her voice, enjoying the stories of her many travels. He was soon laughing at her many anecdotes. God, but she was refreshing. If only they had met under different circumstances ... and if only she wasn't so free-spirited. Perhaps then they might have had a chance of getting to know each other.

Dinner was soon announced. Blackwood guided Mirabella toward the dining room, where an elegant buffet had been laid out on a massive table. Due to Penelope's intervention, Blackwood found himself seated beside the ever-colorful Mirabella. The dinner's conversation centered once more round her travels, and she soon had everyone's attention as she talked of the Far East, of tigers in

Bengal, and of sandstorms raging across hot deserts.

Blackwood silently applauded the lady's inventiveness in dealing with spitting camels, Turkish slaves who yearned to be free, and sultans who wished to heap riches upon her. Only she, he thought, could soothe mighty sultans, and single-handedly lead a dozen slaves to the Turkish border. Blackwood was impressed.

After dinner, Mirabella was surrounded by a bevy of fascinated guests. More than a few of the gentlemen begged to have the first dance of the evening with her—Lord Warwick included.

Blackwood frowned as she allowed the crush of gentlemen to lead her away. He retreated to the sidelines, leaning one arm atop the marble mantelpiece as she was swept into one dance after another by her many admirers. His thoughts darkened as each dance ended and another began.

Mirabella didn't need to look at Lord Blackwood to know that he watched her every move. She felt the heat of his gaze as surely as she would the hot sear of a firebrand. That he bothered to concern himself with her at all was a mystery. She knew without a doubt that Blackwood was not the sort of fellow to become instantly smitten with a woman—as were so many of the gentlemen Mirabella had encountered. He might want a wife to produce an heir; however, he clearly had no need of a dowry, and she could not fathom why he persisted in watching her like a hawk. She told herself he was simply still simmering over the incident with Haluk. His intense interest was no doubt due to the fact that he wished to set her down a peg or two!

"Miss Bella, might I have a word with you?" It was the Duchess of Ravenscar. She seized the moment to claim Mirabella's attention before the next set began and Mirabella was coaxed onto the dance floor again.

Mirabella pulled her thoughts from Blackwood and gave the duchess a warm smile. "Your grace."

The duchess, flanked by the Countess of Coventry and several ladies of the local gentry, tapped her folded fan atop Mirabella's gloved hand. "I wanted to thank you, my dear, for trying to reunite me with my beloved Max. Though the pup you presented was not Max, I do appreciate your efforts on my behalf." The duchess went on to praise the Earl of Blackwood for his undaunted chivalry in locating her spaniel. "Such a gallant he is," said her grace. "What a tragedy that he returned injured from Waterloo to be told the lady he'd planned to marry and his elder brother, Matthew, had died tragic deaths in his absence."

The smile disappeared from Mirabella's face. She hadn't known. "How horrible," she whispered.

The white-haired Countess of Coventry clicked her tongue. "That isn't the half of it, my dear, not by far! I always knew Matthew and Diana were destined for trouble."

"Trouble?" asked Mirabella, not understanding.

The Duchess of Ravenscar hastened to explain. "Lady Diana became rather, ah ... reckless with her reputation once Christian went off to war."

"Reckless? Pah!" cut in the Countess of Coventry. "The chit blew her good name to Hades! Decided to seduce the brother who held the title, she did—and managed *that* easily enough!" The countess looked straight at Mirabella. "Diana and Matthew died en route to one of their many clandestine meeting places. Their carriage ran afoul of a rut in the road and careened over a cliff and the two of them, clasped in each other's arms, tumbled to their deaths. They were found three days later. The ton was abuzz with the story."

Mirabella digested this information. No wonder Blackwood presented himself as stiff and unfeeling; he'd been dealt a terrible blow.

"His lordship hasn't been the same since," said another of the elderly ladies. "He closed up his Town residence after the burials, then secluded himself in Penelope's guest house. I've heard tell he has become an ogre of late."

"Oh, yes!" breathed a fourth lady, fluttering her fan. "An ogre, to be sure! He cannot abide flirtatiousness in any woman. I fear he believes every female walks the same twisted path that his Lady Diana so brazenly tread!"

Mirabella felt a jolt of misgiving. Had Blackwood erroneously placed her in the same frame as the wanton Lady Diana? Did he view her as nothing more than a flirt? Mirabella felt certain that he did.

"Now, now," the Duchess of Ravenscar said soothingly to her friends. "Christian is not as horrible as he would like the world to believe. I know this to be fact, as he took pains to see my precious Max returned to me! Truly, his only fault is that he has been deplorably spoiled by women who have fawned over him. I must say, it is in his favor that he hasn't taken advantage of his position and seduced the many ladies who have given him more than reason enough to turn his glance their way. As for his sorry choice in choosing Lady Diana, we all know what a consummate actress that she-wolf could be, God rest her soul. Though of noble lineage, she remained true to the bad blood entered into her line decades ago. It is no secret that her great-grandmother harbored a penchant to seduce stable boys! Diana's blood, I gather, was not as blue as she liked to believe!"

Mirabella grew uncomfortable. She did not like being privy to gossip—especially gossip concerning Blackwood.

The Countess of Coventry, however, obviously had no qualms about gossip. "How true," she murmured to the Duchess of Ravenscar. "Blackwood was led astray by Diana, and I do not think he shall suffer being carted down that same lane again. It is my opinion that all he needs is a truly *original* woman, one who has the wherewithal to yank him from his self-imposed exile from Society." She lifted her lorgnette to one myopic eye and studied Mirabella. "Tell me, Miss Darlington, what do you think of Lord Blackwood?"

Sensing matchmaking in the air, Mirabella tried not to act the least bit interested. "He—he has been most attentive to me this evening," she said, which was true enough. *Too* attentive, she added, but did not voice the thought.

The countess was not fooled. She lowered the lorgnette, smiling mischievously. "I find it vastly refreshing that Blackwood has emerged from his cocoon of exile and taken it upon himself to escort you about your homecoming party. One cannot help but wonder how such a thing came to pass, though."

Mirabella was saved from giving an answer when a gentleman appeared at her side. 'Twas the nervous but harmless Lord Robertshaw, a young buck whom Mirabella had met before departing for Bengal. He was dressed in cream-colored breeches and a superbly cut mulberry coat. He appeared every inch the fashionable gentleman with his intricately tied neckcloth that sported a sapphire stickpin. Mirabella, however, knew Robertshaw to be shy and anxious. His face burned a bright red all the way to the roots of his sandy hair as he asked her to dance the next set with him.

Though weary of dancing, Mirabella did not have the heart to deny him. Too, accepting Robertshaw's request would spare her from enduring another moment of the Countess of Coventry's shrewd and penetrating stare. Her decision made, Mirabella excused herself from the ladies and allowed Robertshaw to lead her onto the dance floor. She did not miss the fact that Lord Blackwood, standing in the shadows of the ballroom, watched her with a hooded gaze.

Robertshaw proved to be an over-enthusiastic dancer. He continually stepped on Mirabella's toes, his flushed face burning ever brighter.

"Forgive me!" he gasped, stepping yet again on her slippered feet. "I am a woeful dancer, I fear."

Mirabella forced her thoughts from Blackwood long enough to give the gentleman a reassuring smile. "At least you keep steady time, my lord," she replied, hoping to soothe him. She knew she wasn't exactly gliding smoothly about the floor either; Blackwood's heated stare was becoming more than she could bear. Mirabella tried to concentrate on the strains of music as Robertshaw stiffly twirled her about the ballroom. She failed miserably, her left foot tangling with his as the two of them waltzed past Blackwood.

"Oh!" murmured Mirabella, meeting Blackwood's hot gaze just before Robertshaw whirled her about and stepped again on her toe. Over her dance partner's shoulder she saw Blackwood send her a mighty scowl as Robertshaw clasped one arm tighter about her trim waist and attempted to keep her upright.

"My apologies!" gasped Robertshaw, clearly thinking he'd been the total cause of the mishap. "This is all my fault! I—I did not hurt you, did I?"

The Unmatchable Miss Mirabella 87

Mirabella, trying her best to ignore Blackwood (and the stinging pain of her bruised toes), gave Robertshaw a winning smile. "Not at all, my lord. And you are not totally at fault. I simply lost my train of thought."

They waltzed on, leaving Blackwood at the far end of the room. At long last, the music ended. Robertshaw did not immediately release Mirabella from his too-tight hold.

"Please," he begged, "allow me to redeem myself in your eyes. I—I assure you I am much more at ease away from a dance floor. Will you join me for a p-picnic lunch, Miss Darlington? Say d-day after tomorrow? Noonish?"

It was on the tip of Mirabella's tongue to decline the invitation, since Robertshaw was clearly smitten with her; to accept the offer would naturally encourage him to pursue her. It would be cruel to give him false hope. But he held her so tightly, and was so obviously praying she would accept, that Mirabella found she hadn't the heart to deny the request. What would it cost her to join him for an hour or two? Properly chaperoned, of course. She could easily keep their conversation light during the picnic, and could let it be known (gently, of course) that she did not desire his courtship.

"A picnic lunch would be pleasant," she said.

Robertshaw beamed, clutching her tighter still. "Wonderful!" he exclaimed, forgetting himself and nearly squeezing the breath from her.

It was then that Haluk presented himself at Mirabella's side, whispering into her ear. Robertshaw immediately released Mirabella, stepped back, and gave her a deep bow. He retreated with the promise that he would soon meet her for the promised picnic.

Blackwood, meanwhile, had been watching from the far side of the ballroom. In his opinion, young Robertshaw was being much too forward with Mirabella. Blackwood had moved away from the marble mantelpiece, intending to intervene and pull Mirabella away from Robertshaw, when Haluk, the Turk who had toppled him on the knoll, had stepped toward Mirabella and whispered something in her ear. Mirabella then followed her servant out of the room. A frowning Blackwood was not far behind them.

Mirabella's heart beat a wild tattoo as she followed Haluk to a small sitting room at the front of the house. Someone was waiting there, someone who'd demanded to meet her, someone who would not leave without seeing her. To her dismay, she found that that someone was the Gypsy she'd met at the fair earlier. There came a resounding crash as the Gypsy tried—and failed—to lay hands on a dusty violin atop her godmama's cabinet of fine breakables.

Mirabella entered the sitting room just as the Gypsy snapped to attention. He was perched atop the window seat at the far end of the room, a shabby greatcoat folded on the cushions beside him and the cabinet of fine breakables face-down on the floor in front of him.

"'Twas the violin!" declared the Gypsy upon seeing the Turk and Mirabella framed in the doorway. "I thought only to take down the fine instrument and play a song that would bring the lovely lady to my side!"

He held up the violin, then placed it beneath his chin and coaxed an arpeggio from its strings with the bow.

None too pleasantly, Haluk said, "The lady has arrived, sir. Now what?"

"I shall introduce myself, of course!"

The Gypsy placed the violin and bow atop his

greatcoat, then jumped down from the window seat, crunching glass beneath his scuffed boots.

He bowed in Mirabella's direction, a gesture which caused the ends of the blood-red scarf about his neck and the yellow sash about his waist to flutter wildly. He then righted himself, casting both Mirabella and Haluk a brilliant and charming grin that showed to advantage his even, white teeth.

"I am Tomislav Karoly Jozsef Vilaghy!" he proclaimed. "I am in love! Prepare to fall equally in love with me!"

Haluk, slack-jawed, gaped at the man.

Mirabella smothered a giggle. "You can relax, Haluk. I have met the man before."

The Turk heaved a great sigh of relief.

Mirabella smiled.

The Gypsy's proclamation was unbelievable. She suggested to Haluk that he stand guard at the open door, thus appealing to Haluk's sense of propriety as well as to his disdainful desire to stay as far away from the Gypsy as he possibly could.

Gathering her wits, Mirabella entered the room.

"Sir," she said, extending one hand in greeting.

"I, Tomislav Karoly Jozsef Vilaghy, am at your service, my precious lady!"

The Gypsy sketched a deep bow over her outstretched hand. He pressed a soft kiss to the back, all the while gazing deeply into her eyes.

She removed her hand from his and motioned him away from the fallen cabinet. The two of them retired to the sofa whereupon the Gypsy began expounding on the virtues of the violin.

Then he declared: "I would like to play you a love song!"

"Whatever for?" asked Mirabella. "You barely know me."

The Gypsy smiled knowingly. "Love, she comes

on the breeze. She sweeps you away. She makes no excuses. I need not know you. I need only to view you!"

"And so you think you are in love with me."

"I, Tomislav Karoly Jozsef Vilaghy, *know* that I am in love with you!"

He moved off the sofa then and hunkered down on bended knee before her.

Mirabella inwardly groaned. "Oh! Not another proposal, please."

The overzealous Gypsy happily ignored her words. His smile was wide, his dark eyes full of passion.

"Say that you love me, my precious lady! Say you will marry me!"

"Sir, you are far too fervent, not to mention forward. How can I love you when I barely know you?"

"Love is like fortune. She smiles on a person when they least expect it! She has smiled on me ... she will soon smile upon you!"

Indeed? thought Mirabella.

Though she did not wish to break the man's heart, she *did* wish to take leave of him. All this talk of instantaneous love was vexing for one who did not believe in such a thing.

"Pray, do no be hurt, but I am not in love with you, sir."

"I, Tomislav Karoly Jozsef Vilaghy, take no offense," he declared. "Only think of the joy we shall share once you *do* know me!" He reached for her hand, drawing it swiftly to his chest.

Mirabella, unprepared for this action, found herself hard-pressed not to be physically pulled off the sofa. She groped with her free hand for a sturdy hold and found it in the form of one of the sofa's legs. She braced herself lest the man drag her into his arms.

"You feel it, no?" cried the Gypsy, blissfully unaware of the awkward physical position he'd thrust her into. "My heart, she beats with love for you! Can you not feel it, my precious lady? Say that you can!"

What Mirabella *did* feel was the hardness of the man's obviously well-muscled chest and—Zeus and Minerva!—the feel of it brought to mind the moment Lord Blackwood had taken her into his embrace and led her away from a long line of piglets. The feel of him had been firm, and though she was loath to admit it, she had actually felt safe in his arms ...

Good Lord, why had she thought of *him?* And why in the devil had she allowed her meeting with the Gypsy to get so far out of hand?

"Sir," Mirabella began, prepared to order the Gypsy to release her hand and be on his way. But he was gazing up at her with such heart-felt passion that Mirabella hated to be the one to dash his firm belief in love at first sight.

In place of the brusque words she'd intended, she said instead, rather lamely, "I—I do believe I can feel the beat of your heart. And my, but yes, it—it does seem to be beating rather fast ..."

She inwardly winced at her own ill attempt to make any sense whatsoever, but the Gypsy did not seem to mind her ridiculous words.

"Ah, my heart, she is overflowing with love for you!" he exclaimed.

"Yes, well, ahem, you did mention that already."

She resorted to pulling (nay, yanking!) her hand free from his overexuberant hold. That done, she settled back on the sofa, hoping the man would take the hint and get off his blasted knee.

Unfortunately, he did not. Instead, he threw himself into yet another long-winded litany about his undying love for her. He talked of taking her around the world, of sharing hot, sultry nights with her, and of what he, ever an attentive lover, could teach her.

Mirabella, her cheeks flaming at his bold words, decided enough was enough.

"Forgive me, sir, but though your attentions are ... flattering, I—I cannot possibly return your love. You see I am—"

"Spoken for!" he interrupted before she could utter another word. "I know! I watch you and your lover at the fair. From afar, I see the smoldering passion in his eyes! Ah! My heart, she did break to see him take you in his arms!"

Mirabella blinked in astonishment. The Gypsy had seen *passion* in Lord Blackwood's gaze? Oh, for the love of—

" 'Tis no matter, though!" the man cried, suddenly jumping to his feet. "I, Tomislav Karoly Jozsef Vilaghy, adore a challenge!" Hands on hips, he straightened to his full height and announced, "From this moment forward, I shall commence to make you mine! I shall turn your thoughts away from your lover! I shall make you forget he even exists!"

He swept her a deep bow and then turned and headed for the window seat upon which he'd been perched when Mirabella had first entered the room.

To Mirabella's dismay, he bounded atop the cushions and then neatly unlatched the windows. He thrust them open, allowing a healthy breeze to rush inside the room. The breeze ruffled the ends of his long, dark hair and played havoc with his brightly colored sash and neckerchief, and with Penelope's sheer curtains as well. He gave a sharp whistle—hailing what, Mirabella had no idea!

Legs spread and arms akimbo, the Gypsy sent Mirabella one last, longing look.

"I, Tomislav Karoly Jozsef Vilaghy, bid you farewell. But I shall return. Until then, my precious lady, prepare to fall in love!"

Mirabella decided she'd doubtless ruin the effect of his departure should she mumble a good-bye. Instead, she merely gave a small wave of her hand.

The Gypsy sent her a rakish grin.

In spite of herself, she felt the corners of her mouth turn up into a smile.

And then the Gypsy reached down to gather up his greatcoat, blew a kiss in her direction, and jumped out of the window to the ground below.

Mirabella's curiosity got the best of her. She'd never met a Gypsy before, and certainly not one who came and went via the window!

She leaned on the window seat and saw that the Gypsy had been whistling for his mount. A well-trained (and unsaddled) horse could be seen spiriting the Gypsy off into the distance.

"That one is trouble," muttered Haluk, who'd come up behind Mirabella and was peering with her out the window.

"Indeed," agreed Mirabella.

Together, they watched until the Gypsy and his horse disappeared into the night.

What a day this had been! And to think she had yet to endure the remainder of her godmama's party—a party that would, no doubt, bring her into further contact with Lord Blackwood.

"Haluk," said Mirabella.

"Yes, Miss Bella?"

"Remind me never to go to a fair again, will you?"

"Yes, Miss Bella."

It was then Mirabella looked down at the cushions of the window seat and noticed that Penelope's violin and bow were nowhere in sight.

The Gypsy had stolen them!

"And Haluk," said Mirabella, "I think you'd best go and count the silver, and mayhap even my gems."

8

Blackwood was waylaid by an old acquaintance before he was able to follow Mirabella and her servant to a small sitting room at the front of the house. He was aghast to find her entertaining the Gypsy from the fair. He stepped into the room just as the Gypsy exited through the windows.

"Faith!" muttered Blackwood, the sound of his voice causing Mirabella to face him. "You should have known better than to speak again with that overzealous man!"

Mirabella flashed him a withering glance. "You, sir," she said, "have no business dogging my every step!" With a regal toss of her head, she moved past him out of the room, leaving him to deal with the towering Turk.

The man called Haluk glared at him. Blackwood grinned. "Rest easy, my man," he said. "I wish only to see that your mistress doesn't kick up the dust—and God knows that Lord Warwick will prove trouble enough for her." With that, Blackwood slipped away, leaving a bemused Haluk staring after him.

Blackwood returned to the ballroom only to find Mirabella surrounded by suitors. A sea of fashionable and elegant gentlemen moved about her. She spoke at length with one flushed-face buck—a Lord Robertshaw—and Blackwood deduced within an instant that the young Robertshaw was

95

smitten with her. But Mirabella did not seem to notice. She allowed herself to be thrust into one dance after another: a polonaise, a minuet, several country dances, and a cotillion.

Blackwood frowned, nursed his glass of brandy, and stared at her all the while. He did not like that Mirabella was such a flirt that she'd permitted numerous bucks to dance with her. She was, by far, too reckless for her own good! He set down his glass and approached her as the musicians began a waltz. Pity that Lord Montague Warwick moved toward her as well.

Warwick managed to sweep her into the middle of the ballroom first. Blackwood's gaze darkened as Lord Monty whispered something into Mirabella's ear. *Damn!* thought Blackwood. He'd been but a moment too late . . .

Mirabella tried not to frown as Lord Monty claimed her for the waltz. She would have much preferred sitting out this number. But Lord Monty proved a most insistent admirer, and Mirabella, enraged by Blackwood's inference that she was a tad too risqué, thought to teach his lordship a lesson that she wasn't one to conform to the rules of Society. Unfortunately, that lesson was proving to be at her own expense. She was near smothering beneath Lord Monty's attention and his whispered demand that she join him for a morning's ride the next day when Blackwood, his face a mask of rage, interrupted their waltz.

"I believe I shall dance with the lady," he said, surprising Mirabella, and probably everyone else in the room. He didn't care.

"I think not," replied Warwick.

"Think again," Blackwood said, reaching for Mirabella's right hand and pulling her away.

Mirabella went willingly enough, but only because she did not wish to cause a public scandal. She watched as Lord Monty's face whirled away from view. "What a perfect devil you are," she told Blackwood.

"I've been termed worse."

"I am sure you have!"

"But I am not," he said, "the devil you paint me."

"No?"

"No," he said, and then danced her toward the outer reaches of the ballroom. "Unlike Warwick, I will not pursue you only because of the size of your purse. And unlike your many other suitors, I will not seek your favor only because you are fair of face and a true original."

Mirabella pulled away from him. "So why *are* you dancing with me, my lord?" she demanded.

He hesitated only a moment. "Because I can do no less," he answered, leading her out through the French doors and onto the stone terrace beyond. "And because I wish to keep you away from the wily Lord Warwick. He is not worthy of your attentions."

Mirabella simmered. "Pray, my lord, allow me to deem who is and who is not worthy of my attentions!"

"I would," he said, "if but for the fact that I think you are far too spirited to make that choice."

Darkness closed around them. A part of her thought him kind in worrying over her welfare, while another part of her balked at his audacity in implying that she couldn't take care of herself.

"I have no need of a gallant knight to save me from the jaws of improper conduct, my lord," she said.

"No?" he breathed, his handsome face too close to hers. "Does that mean you are always such a flirt, Miss Darlington?"

Mirabella thought to bring him down a peg or two. "Perhaps you, sir, are more a rogue than a knight." She met his stormy gaze in the moonlight, and knew a strong urge to thwart him, to tell him that she planned to join Lord Monty for a ride come morning, and that she intended to share a picnic lunch with young Lord Robertshaw. Though she did not mind promising Warwick a ride since she was sure she would have no trouble managing him, she had not been comfortable accepting Lord Robertshaw's invitation. The young man was not of Warwick's ilk, nor even Blackwood's. He was but a young buck, still wet behind the ears. Mirabella decided that she would be kind to the gentleman and discourage further pursuit from him. But Lord Blackwood need not know that.

"I will flirt when and with whom I please, Lord Blackwood," she added. "If that includes a morning ride with Lord Warwick and an afternoon picnic with Lord Robertshaw, it is no concern of yours." With that, she pulled away from him and hurried back into the house.

Blackwood frowned after her. "Over my dead body," he whispered.

Mirabella rose early the next morning, though she hadn't gone to bed until well after midnight. The party had gone on and on, with young Lord Robertshaw making a great fuss over her. He'd gotten well into his cups somewhere near eleven o'clock and had begun toasting Mirabella's eyelashes. Lord Warwick had pursued her in quite a different way. No pretty, frivolous phrases for him. He'd courted her with just a brush of his arm against hers, a private smile from across the room. Mirabella knew she was treading dangerous territory in agreeing to ride with him this morning.

But her outrage at Blackwood and her own stubborn pride had pressed her to tell Blackwood she'd accepted Warwick's invitation.

Blackwood.

Just thinking of the man made her blood boil—and yes, she admitted, caused butterflies to flutter within her stomach. *He* had not courted her. No, none of that for the always cool, always in command Lord Blackwood. He had stood apart from the other guests, his dark, brooding gaze following her as she'd danced and later as she'd chatted with old friends. And then he'd sought her out only to give her a tongue-lashing for what he deemed her outrageous behavior.

What nerve he had in claiming she was a flirt! She should have slapped him—but then, had she done so, she could only guess at what might have transpired. His lordship was far more volatile than any man she'd ever encountered. There was a palatable force shimmering within him, one that could be unleashed with the slightest provocation, she knew. His passions, so intense, were a powder keg waiting to be ignited, a hurricane brewing on a distant horizon. He could be fiery-hot one minute, ice-cold the next. And yet, there was a part of him, she hazarded, that no one—perhaps not even he himself—understood, a part of him that could be as gentle as a spring rain, as heartbreakingly honest as a child's laughter. Given time, Mirabella thought she might be able to thaw the ice encrusting his heart, might be able to penetrate the aloofness that had been bred in him.

Not that it mattered. She suspected she was never going to see Lord Blackwood again. He would doubtless retreat to the guest house and lock himself inside the place, do whatever it was a reclusive lord did. She'd angered him last night. She'd pushed him too far. And he had pushed her too hard—for here she was, spending a morning with Lord Warwick.

Mirabella rang for Annie to come and help her dress. She waited a full fifteen minutes before she deduced that Annie had no doubt nipped a bit too much of Aunt Nellie's gin last night. The maid was probably still sound asleep. She decided to take care of her own toilette.

Mirabella dressed herself in a smart riding habit of bright violet. She pulled her hair up into a loose chignon. One curl, however, refused to be pinned, and so she allowed it to dangle tantalizingly along the column of her throat. She adjusted her violet hat with its single white plume, pulled on soft kidskin gloves, and then hastened downstairs and outside.

The morning was gloriously refreshing. The rising sun had yet to burn away the last traces of fog that hung in ribbons across the land. She could hear Aunt Nellie's peafowl and several geese honking in the distance. What a beautiful day! Perhaps her morning's ride with Lord Warwick would not prove an unwise decision after all. Surely Blackwood had exaggerated when he'd described Lord Warwick's unsavoriness.

Mirabella frowned. Now why did her mind persist in thinking of Blackwood? She'd do better to forget him. But as she rounded the graveled drive, she espied not Lord Warwick awaiting her arrival outside the stables, but Blackwood!

He stood tall and handsome betwixt two beautiful black mounts. He held the horses' reins loosely in one hand, his gloves in the other. He was dressed for riding, she noted, his fawn-colored breeches showing to great advantage the lean musculature of his legs, his black boots polished to a glossy shine, his white lawn shirt and impeccable neckcloth a startling contrast to his dark hair and obsidian gaze.

"You!" Mirabella gasped.

He reached up with one hand and tipped his hat, though his gesture of greeting did not include a smile. "And good morning to you, too."

That he intended a morning's ride—with a partner to accompany him—was obvious. An alarm rang in her head. Her eyes narrowing suspiciously, she said, "I have come to meet Lord Warwick."

"I know," he said, his voice grim.

"*And?*"

"And?" he repeated.

Mirabella grew impatient. "Have you seen him, my lord?"

"Perhaps."

Mirabella snapped her riding crop against her skirts in exasperation, then turned toward the stables.

"I wouldn't bother looking for the gentleman in there."

Mirabella glared at Blackwood. "Why is that, my lord?" she demanded.

Blackwood rocked back on his heels, nonchalantly tipping his face up to capture the pale rays of the rising sun. "Because he isn't there."

"And where *is* he?"

Blackwood shrugged. "How the deuce should I know? I don't make a habit of keeping myself informed of Warwick's comings and goings."

Clearly, the man's surliness of the night before had not abated. Mirabella gnashed her teeth. She wouldn't allow the man to goad her. That was what he wanted. He wished to torment her, nothing more. She whirled about, intending to head back to the house and await Lord Warwick there. He *would* come searching for her, eventually—no matter what Blackwood might have done to thwart their morning's ride.

"Then I shall wait for him at the house," she announced.

"No," he said curtly, abruptly. "If you intend to ride this morning, Miss Darlington, you shall ride with me."

Angered by his assumption that she would join him, just like that, without so much as a by-your-leave, Mirabella turned to face him. "What an overblown opinion of yourself you harbor, my lord. Do you actually think I would ride anywhere with you after your insufferable behavior last night?"

"I sought only to play your knight."

"I had no need of your assistance."

"That is not how I viewed the situation. You nearly started a riot with that low-cut, clinging gown of yours. 'Twas bold of you to dampen your petticoats," he added, his voice rich and low. "At the very least, you could have worn some lace to fill in the bodice."

Mirabella, fighting down a tiny, purely female thrill at the fact that he'd even noticed her apparel last night, stiffened. "I am, my lord, past the age when it is necessary to tuck in concealing lace. And might I add, a *true gentleman* would not dare comment on my lack of lace, or—or . . ."

"The dampness of your petticoats?" His black eyes smoldered as he speared her with an intense gaze. "How fortunate for me, then, that you deem me a rogue. Rogues, I hear, are forgiven a great many transgressions."

How rude of him to remind her of the word she'd so carelessly flung at him last night. "You, my lord, are forgiven nothing."

His lips straightened into a taut, unyielding line. "It isn't your forgiveness I seek." With a click of his tongue, he led the horses toward Mirabella. "You will ride with me, Miss Darlington, and I shall see that we have proper escort."

He wasn't asking her, but rather commanding her. Mirabella noted those audacious black eyes, the tightness pulling at the corners of his too-sensual mouth. She recalled what the Duchess of Ravenscar had said about him last night, that he was accustomed to women doing his bidding, that he'd been deplorably spoiled by a great many women throughout his life. He'd rarely been denied—if ever. Obviously he arrogantly assumed every woman would bend to his will. Well, here was one who would not!

"I think not," Mirabella said. "I have promised my morning to Lord Warwick."

Blackwood's gaze turned wintery. His hands gripped hard on the reins. "What else did you promise him, Miss Darlington?"

"I don't see where that is any concern of yours, my lord." Mirabella would have turned away from him, but he took a step forward, and halted just a heartbeat from her.

"Tell me. What exactly *did* you promise Warwick?"

"You—you are crowding me, my lord,"' said Mirabella, taking a wary step back.

He advanced yet again. "What I should do is shake you soundly. Don't you realize what an animal Warwick can be?"

"Lord Warwick has been nothing but kind to me," she replied, trying but failing to put some distance between them. The toes of their leather boots touched; she could sense the heat of the man, could smell the clean, masculine scent of him wafting about her.

"If that cad is *kind*, then I am a bloody saint."

"H-hardly," managed Mirabella. "You, sir are an ogre."

"Only when I need to be." He leaned closer still.

He was very tall and broad, and the energy in him, the intensity, seemed to pour out of his body and flow into hers. Mirabella felt herself a powerless being, one enslaved by emotions she feared to acknowledge.

"I'd be a fool to let you go trailing after Warwick," Blackwood muttered.

Mirabella felt his warm breath flutter across her cheekbone. She had to force herself not to tremble at the sensation. "You—you have no say in the matter, my lord."

"No?"

"None whatsoever." She lifted her chin in defiance, challenging him to gainsay her.

"His courtship will lead you to disaster."

"I—I have hardly invited the man to court me."

"If that is what you believe, then you have obviously been too long absent from gentle Society. Allow me to refresh your memory," he said, his black gaze burning into hers, searing her soul. He hadn't so much as touched her, yet Mirabella felt as though he'd pulled her into his embrace, he was staring at her so intently. "A lady does not go riding alone with a gentleman lest she hopes to invite further attention from him."

"Thank you for that reminder, my lord. Enlightened as you are, I trust you'll understand why I shan't ride anywhere with you, then!" She couldn't keep the sarcasm from her voice. She needn't have worried about it, though, for Blackwood deliberately ignored her tone.

" 'Tis a reckless path, accepting Warwick's invitation," he continued. "He is little more than a skirt-chaser. He makes a game of wooing and then discarding women. I choose not to believe that you, Miss Darlington, would fall so easily into his trap. I'd thought you beyond all that, a wordly woman who would not suffer his antics."

His words stung. Mirabella knew very well what type of man Warwick was; she had been dodging his kind for years, and she'd prided herself on the fact that she'd not been swayed by any of them. Until now. If not for Blackwood's arrogant intervention, she'd never have looked twice at Lord Warwick. That fact did not sit well with her.

"But you had thought me to suffer *your* antics?" she demanded.

"I am hardly of Warwick's ilk."

"There are those who would argue that, my lord."

"Let them argue away. What concerns me at the moment is your foolish intention to be courted by the likes of him."

"I simply agreed to join him for a morning's ride—"

"Alone, no less. I suppose you shall next inform me that you have not only ceased to worry about tucking lace but have also decided you have no need of a chaperone!"

Mirabella gave a stubborn nod in answer.

Blackwood frowned. "You, Miss Darlington, are too beautiful *not* to have a chaperone."

Mirabella opened her mouth and then shut it just as quickly. She would not respond to him. She wouldn't. That was what he wanted, expected. If he thought she was like all the other women in his life who had so freely blushed at his compliments (if indeed he meant his words as a compliment!), he was wrong.

"Admit to me you have your doubts about Warwick," Blackwood said, his voice low, throbbing. "You're debating whether or not you should wait for him, whether you should even trust him to be alone with you. You are a very passionate woman, Miss Darlington, and there is nothing Warwick enjoys more than passion in his women."

Mirabella's cheeks flamed. "What I am debating, my lord, is whether or not I should slap your face for such impertinence!"

"But you won't."

"I assure you, my palm is itching to do so."

"I mean to ensure that you won't ride alone with Warwick."

Mirabella gazed directly into those fathomless black eyes that could sap the very strength from her. "How can you be so certain, my lord?"

"Warwick isn't the type of man you desire."

She flinched at the utter certainty of his words. "And—and what makes you think I—I desire any man at all?"

A moment of silence welled between them ... and then, softly, with unflagging assurance, he said, "Because in that musty tent at the fair, you shared with me your innermost thoughts concerning the type of man you seek."

Mirabella felt the hot sear of embarrassment burn through her. "I—I was talking of a spaniel, not a—a man."

Blackwood seemed not to have heard her. "You haven't met the type of man you seek—or rather, you do not think you have."

He stood just a breath away, a soft breeze ruffling a lock of black hair that splayed down across his forehead beneath the brim of his hat. His eyes were like granite. He reached out, capturing her right wrist in one strong hand. His fingers curled about it, his thumb seeking the place where her pulse beat a frantic rhythm. Gentle, he traced a pattern of tiny whorls there. "Warwick has a way of making a woman feel as though she and she alone is the reason the sun rises and sets," Blackwood said.

Mirabella felt the heat of him steal through the soft kid of her glove. It took every ounce of her strength not to melt at the hot sensations now stabbing through her.

"I—I am not so naive, my lord."

"Then why bother with Warwick at all?"

Because of my damnable pride, she thought. *Because you pushed me too far on the terrace last night . . . and because a part of me wishes to make you jealous.* It was the latter thought that troubled her most of all.

Blackwood's thumb moved up, slipped beneath the cuff of her blouse. He caressed a path deep beneath her sleeve, his thumb warm, slightly calloused. Mirabella sucked in a ragged breath, trying—but failing—to stop the trembling of her body.

"Promise me you'll not go off alone with Warwick," he said.

"I don't know why you're making such a fuss—"

"I'm not making a fuss. 'Tis a demand, pure and simple. Say it. Tell me you'll not give Warwick the chance to court you."

"How very like you, my lord, to demand something of me!" Mirabella drew her arm away from him, felt his thumb slide, hot and slow, down the inside of her wrist. A shiver skidded down her spine. "P-perhaps," she said, far too breathlessly for her own comfort, "it isn't Lord Warwick I should be wary of, but you."

His gaze locked with hers. "I am nothing like him."

I know, thought Mirabella, *and that is the problem.* She could manage the Lord Warwicks of the world. She'd been dealing with them all of her adult life. Blackwood, however, was an enigma to her. She turned away from him.

"Where are you going?" he demanded.

"Back to the house, to await Lord Warwick," Mirabella said, surprised at how difficult it was to get the words out. She managed three steps before Blackwood spoke again.

"He won't be coming for you. I've made certain of that."

Mirabella went cold. She stopped and glanced at him over one shoulder.

After a pregnant pause, he elaborated. "I told Warwick you won't be riding with him this morning—nor any morning, for that matter. I made it clear that the two of us are ... smitten with each other. I told Warwick we plan to marry before the end of the summer. He believed me, of course. I can be convincing when the mood takes me." Blackwood motioned with just a nod of his head toward a trampled path snaking off into a distant field. "He departed ten minutes before you arrived."

Mirabella pivoted to face him, her fists clenched tight at her sides. How dare he! "I do not believe that I have ever disliked any man as much as I do you at this moment, my lord."

A lone muscle twitched along his strong jawline. "Far better for you to despise me than to be debauched by Warwick," he said, his voice clipped.

"I am capable of taking care of my own self, sir."

"I disagree, Miss Darlington. It is my opinion that someone needs to take a firm hand where you are concerned. You've thumbed your nose at propriety one too many times. Your flirtatious, impish ways will only land you in trouble."

Flirtatious? *Impish?* Oh, but he had gone too far! "I am not of a mind to have you ring a peal over me, my lord. I cannot, nor have I ever, tolerated authority figures. You may save your lecture for someone who'll listen!"

"Perhaps," he said darkly, "it is time you changed your ways."

Mirabella had had quite enough of his arrogance. So he though he could just step in and meddle in her life, did he? Well, he was wrong!

In a fury, she snatched up the reins of one of the horses from him, pulled the mount round, then heaved herself up onto the sidesaddle. She didn't bother to rearrange her skirts, or even to settle herself properly. Instead, she turned the beast toward the open field.

"What the deuce do you think you're doing?" Blackwood demanded, making a motion for the reins and causing her horse to shy to one side.

Mirabella simultaneously calmed the spirited horse and yanked the reins from Lord Blackwood's reach. "I am going to find Lord Warwick," she snapped. "Now kindly step out of my way, sir!"

"The devil I will," Blackwood growled. "I'll not allow you to become so much unmolded clay in Warwick's blackened hands!" He planted himself firmly in front of her, feet spread wide on the graveled drive, arms akimbo.

Mirabella ignored the warning in his eyes, ignored the fact that he posed a human barrier in front of her. She'd race past him or she'd be damned. Imagine, him telling Warwick the two of them would soon marry! What audacity! What utter arrogance!

"I promised Lord Warwick a morning's ride," Mirabella said to him through gritted teeth. "I am, if nothing else, my lord, a woman of my word."

So saying, she abruptly gave a signal to her

mount. The horse leaped forward and to the right. She allowed the beast its head, and then, in a clatter of hooves, she left a fuming Lord Blackwood in a cloud of dust.

9

His lordship was forced to stumble back a step as Mirabella charged past him, headed round the stable, and then sped like lightning toward the path Warwick had taken.

"Damnation!" he cursed.

What had begun as a noble gesture of trying to safeguard the virtue of Penelope's goddaughter had somehow become a thoroughly muddled affair. So much for chivalry. The little imp hadn't so much as thanked him for intervening. Instead, she'd had the nerve to snap at him, accusing him of presenting himself as a smothering, authoritative figure.

"Zounds," muttered Blackwood, none too happily. As he saw it, he had two choices. He could allow the high-strung Miss Darlington to simmer in her own stew and face a morning's ride alone with Warwick. Or he could race after her and try to speak some reason to her. Not that she'd listen to reason—at least, not his. She'd made it clear she wanted nothing more to do with him.

Mounting his own horse, Blackwood considered riding in the opposite direction. If Miss Darlington was so bent on throwing caution—as well as her reputation—to the wind, who was he to intervene? But he could not desert her now.

He glanced at the path she'd taken. There, in the distance, he could see her, riding fast for the top of the grassy knoll. Her white plume bobbed, her violet habit vivid against the fog. In an instant, he perceived that she wasn't sitting quite right in the saddle, that she was fighting to stay seated at all. She'd picked that horse because it had a sidesaddle—luck would have it that he put a sidesaddle on the more spirited of the horses. Just as Blackwood wondered if he should linger long enough to see that she made it to the top of the knoll, the horse beneath her suddenly reared. Its front hooves clawed the air, a sharp whinny of fright issued forth and echoed across the lands. The lady was thrust forcibly to the side just as the beast came down on all fours and darted to the left, racing pell-mell into the open pasture where Penelope's sheep grazed.

Blackwood did not hesitate. He spurred his own mount forward, charging across the graveled drive and onto the path Mirabella had taken. She'd be thrown from the saddle in another moment! He leaned low over the black's neck, fear for Mirabella's safety slicing through him like a sharp blade ... and as his horse made quick work of covering the distance between them, he was suddenly, horribly reminded of that moment when he'd ridden hard into the heat of battle at Waterloo: the wind tunneling about him, the hoofbeats pounding, his heart racing wildly. Wind whipped through his hair, his teeth. His whole body rattled with the thud of his horse's hooves. And then the nightmare of that vicious, frightening battle rushed into his brain, exploding with sounds he'd tried to forget. He heard again the screams of the dying, the belch of cannon fire, the whine of that fateful lead ball that had imbedded itself in his left thigh.

Dread slammed through his body. The very memories he'd been trying to forget were suddenly upon him, sucking him down into a dark, depthless void. *Dear God, not now. Don't let the memories come now, nor ever again.* But they were coming. Fast and furious. Beneath his jacket and fine lawn shirt, Blackwood felt his skin ripple with goose bumps. Fear and anger skipped along every nerve in his body. He set his mouth into a grim line, fought to overcome the tidal wave of too many memories, and set his sights, his thoughts, on Mirabella.

He came abreast of her and the wild-eyed mount halfway down the other side of the grassy hill. She was clinging to the black's mane, the reins wrapped about one slim wrist as she tried, in vain to halt the beast.

"A—a snake, or some such thing, in the grass!" she called, trying to explain why she was now careening out of control.

Blackwood barely heard her. He might have been a world away. He still heard the desperate cries of battle, felt again and again that heart-stopping ball of some faceless Frenchman's lead embed itself in his thigh. He gave a strangled cry, tried hard to banish the memories, but realized, sick at heart, that the images, the pain, would be forever in him. In a fury, he stood in the stirrups, leaned toward Mirabella, and made a grab for her mount's lead. He gave a mighty tug. He was forced roughly to the side, jarring his injured thigh, but managed to slow the beast nonetheless. He guided them to a safe stop, biting back the pain that radiated through him.

"My lord, you've hurt yourself!" Mirabella gasped. She jumped down off the saddle, worry creasing her pretty brow. "Please," she insisted, "play the gallant no more, sir. My godmama has told me of your injury at Waterloo, and I can see for myself that you've jarred your wounded leg."

" 'Tis my *healing* leg," he corrected.

"Of course," murmured Mirabella. "Perhaps a moment of rest would do you well, sir." As soon as he'd dismounted, she ordered him to seat himself upon the grass, then bent down beside him, the reins of the nervous horses held tight in one small fist. "Perhaps if you would stretch out your leg, my lord," she said. "Like this." Brazenly, she took it upon herself to guide his left leg forward with her free hand.

Blackwood drew in a deep breath at the contact of her gentle hand on his burning flesh.

"Have I hurt you, my lord?"

"No," he said, gritting his teeth.

She passed her hand down to his kneecap, worrying over him. "My servant, Haluk, could prepare an ointment for you, my lord, one that would soothe the ache in your leg. If you wish, I could see that you have that ointment by this evening."

She was completely unaware of what her touch was doing to him. She had no inkling that her very nearness unsettled his emotions. Blackwood reached up with his right hand and stilled her frantic motions. "What I wish," he said, fighting against the urge to take her into his arms, "is for you to turn your attentions away from Lord Warwick. Pray, do not follow him, Miss Darlington."

She sat back, frowning. "You worry overly much, my lord. I am not as impressionable as you believe, nor am I so enamored of Lord Warwick as to make a fool of myself over him!"

"Oh?" said Blackwood, unconvinced, still fighting the effects of her nearness. "And is that why you spurred your horse into this pasture and nearly saw the both of us tumbled to the ground? For a woman who is uninterested in Warwick's pursuit, you have certainly made a cake of us both by charging after the gentleman. 'Tis clear to me you think too much of that cad."

Mirabella clicked her tongue, glaring at him, then shot to her feet. "You, sir, haven't a clue as to what I think!" With that, the Unmatchable Miss Mirabella mounted her horse and galloped back down the way she'd come.

Blackwood could only stare after her, wondering what in the devil he'd said that had angered her so. Faith! There was no understanding her.

An hour later, Blackwood muttered a curse and threw his mostly-clothed body into the swirling mineral waters of Penelope's hot spring.

"Damn," he muttered unhappily, his thoughts filled with Mirabella. It wasn't at all like him to be so fixated on a woman. She was like a fever in his blood.

He should have had the good sense to seek the waters in Bath instead of tramping off for the Cotswolds and Penelope's very queer Stormhaven. Perhaps then he might have avoided meeting the Unmatchable Miss Mirabella and thus being plagued by memories of her comely smile and flashing blue eyes.

Then again, thought Blackwood, had he taken the waters at Bath he doubtless would have been deviled by the many acquaintances he had there. God only knew, the Pump Room had become overcrowded of late. Bath had become little more than a place to be seen. There was always a crush at the coffeehouses, and the reading rooms had become places to do *anything* but read. Finding privacy had become nearly impossible.

Blackwood much preferred Stormhaven's isolation. How the deuce Penelope had ever created a hot spring here, though, he had no idea—nor was he of a mind to question her about it. Penelope Barrington could charm the skin from a cobra if she so desired. That she had her own mineral spring was not such an unusual thing, Blackwood supposed.

Penelope had certainly outdone herself in designing the place. It looked like a Grecian temple, with its white marble columns. There were three antechambers, each with its own fountain, where the guests could fill their cups with the mineral water and lounge before or after enjoying the spa waters. The area above the bath itself was opened to the sky.

One might have begun to wonder whether or not Penelope had lived in the time of the Romans, so exquisite was her mineral bath. Lead piping ran beneath the house and ensured the water would indeed be hot. The pool where her guests could partake of the soothing waters was of circular construction, shallow on all sides and eight feet deep at the center. An oasis of white marble seemed to float at the center of the pool, and atop this was a mammoth lion's head, from whose mouth gushed a continuous flow of hot mineral water.

In the afternoon, Penelope provided numerous servants so that her guests would not lack even the smallest of comforts. Floating trays set in the pool were constantly supplied with refreshments, fruits, handkerchiefs for the ladies when it was their turn to take the waters, and snuffboxes for the gentlemen when it was their turn.

In the early-morning hours, and after dark, the spa became Blackwood's own domain.

He leaned his dark head against the smooth marble edge of the pool and closed his eyes. He was finally able to relax. The soothing waters did wonders for the burning in his thigh. Now, if only he could become accustomed to the *smell* of the water—and if only he could get the remembered sight of Mirabella out of his mind, he might yet find some peace!

The Unmatchable Miss Mirabella 117

Alas, Blackwood's brain did not want to cooperate. In his mind's eye he saw again a pair of summery-blue eyes fringed by thick, dusky lashes. The lady's features were ever so pleasing, and her mouth ... that pouty, pretty mouth was made for kissing.

Christ's nails. Would his thoughts never be free of her? 'Twas unbelievable that he, once so adamant never to fall under the spell of another woman, was now plagued by thoughts of a miss he barely knew.

But, ah ... what thoughts they were!

He could very well imagine divesting the lady of her many silks, could imagine taking her svelte body in his arms ...

He threw himself down deeper into the steamy water and allowed his imagination to take flight. God knew he wasn't getting anywhere fighting it.

But just then, he heard a whisper of motion coming from near the door.

Devil take it, could a man not even enjoy a fantasy or two without being interrupted? 'Twas no doubt Haskins come to see if he needed anything.

Without opening his eyes, he said, "Haskins? I thought I told you to take the day off. You're supposed to be enjoying yourself, not trailing after me."

There was no answer. Instead, Blackwood heard the unmistakable sound of the chair upon which he'd draped his coat and neckcloth, shoes and stockings, being knocked over. There followed the clatter of his cane rolling across the marble floor.

"Dammit, Haskins! You know I detest intrusion!"

Blackwood abandoned the image of summery-blue eyes gazing passionately up at him and opened his own eyes.

Haskins was nowhere in sight.

Indeed, there was no other human in the bathhouse at all.

Blackwood sat up, peering through the steam that wafted up from the hot mineral waters.

"Who's there?" he demanded.

Nothing.

And then, much to his dismay, he saw through the mist a pair of large amber-colored eyes. Feline eyes, eyes that were regarding him as though he might prove to be a tasty meal.

Thunderstruck, Blackwood held himself perfectly still for fear of giving the beast any reason to attack. But the animal's only thoughts appeared to be on lapping up a bit of the pool water. Then it loped over to his lordship's fallen clothes, plopped its great weight down upon the pile, and commenced to playfully bat at Blackwood's cane.

"*Gadzooks,*" he muttered. Since when did the Cotswolds harbor tigers?

Then he remembered Penelope's words about having loosed a tiger from its cage.

He'd thought she'd been jesting; obviously, she had not.

Now, why did that not surprise him?

10

Blackwood soon concluded that the animal wasn't going to attack him—at least not at the moment. It was far too interested in gnawing the top of his best rosewood cane. He did not mind; he detested that cane, and all that it represented.

"Gnaw away," he said softly, settling himself comfortably in the hot spring once again.

Though the animal flicked the tip of its long tail at the sound of Blackwood's voice, it did not appear to be concerned by his presence. Indeed, the beast actually regarded his lordship with a rather bored expression.

Blackwood grinned broadly at it.

The tiger blinked large, amber eyes, yawned expansively, then went back to sharpening its fangs on the once-perfect walking stick.

Blackwood knew it would be a difficult walk down to the guest house without his cane, but he wasn't about to scramble out of the pool and wrestle with a tiger over ownership. Not that the beast was full-grown, but a tiger was a tiger, after all.

Blackwood surmised the animal to be no more than six or seven months old. It had yet to grow into its huge paws and large head. Given another few weeks, however, and the animal would become a dangerous predator. Blackwood made a mental note to remind Penelope to return it to its cage and see it on its way.

Of course, there existed the very real possibility

that Penelope hadn't been *able* to recapture the tiger and perhaps that was why the beast was wandering about the grounds. Then again, Penelope was such an odd sort that she might think it a grand lark to have a tiger running loose—barring, of course, any more incidents with hapless spaniels! Too, her peafowl in the northern part of the gardens would doubtless prove fair game to a young tiger.

So thinking, Blackwood decided he should at least attempt to keep the tiger secluded in one of the bathhouse's antechambers. That done, he could inquire of Penelope as to what she wanted done with the animal.

Pity he hadn't any raw meat with which to lure the beast. Perhaps the cane would prove suitable enough.

With that in mind, he slipped slowly beneath the waters and swam toward the opposite side of the pool. He surfaced carefully, mindful not to move too swiftly. He raised his head up near the marble edging and peered over it.

The tiger was very much aware of his close proximity, but it merely flopped over onto its back. It rubbed its spine into Blackwood's clothes and kicked its legs into the air like a playful kitten.

"Weston would be highly insulted," Blackwood told the tiger.

The animal let forth a half-growl that became a deep, rumbling purr. It had managed to entangle its forepaws in Blackwood's neckcloth. The beast clawed at the thing, then nipped halfheartedly at it, thoroughly ruining the starched linen.

"Ah," whispered Blackwood, smiling, "now you've gone and insulted my manservant, Haskins, as well. He has nightmares about my neckcloths, I swear. Nasty things, neckcloths; a constant plague for a gentlemen such as myself who are all thumbs. Carry on, good fellow, carry on."

The tiger did just that. It also rolled and rubbed so much that his lordship's expensive coat was soon muddied.

Blackwood made a motion to hoist himself out of the pool and attempt to lure the tiger into one of the antechambers with the cane as bait. But there suddenly came a resounding crash from the front entrance.

"Zeus and Minerva!" a very feminine voice muttered.

Blackwood instantly recognized that voice. "Ah ... we've company," he told the tiger. "Lest I be accused of not giving you fair warning, the lady is fetching. Beautiful, in fact. Try to keep your tongue behind your teeth, will you? God knows I'll be hard-pressed to do likewise."

The beast, however, had already leaped to its feet, and before Blackwood could even decide whether or not he'd be forced to stand before the tiger and safeguard the intruder, the animal bounded between the nearest twin columns.

It quickly sprinted off, leaving a trail of his lordship's clothes behind ... and banging Blackwood's cane—held tight in its mouth—on the marble flooring as it went.

Blackwood muttered a soft curse and watched through rising mists of steam as the woman who'd plagued his thoughts came hobbling into the room.

The fetching Mirabella appeared fit to be tied, what with her enchanting blue eyes flashing daggers and her pouty mouth schooled into a deep frown. Blackwood hazarded (by the resounding crash he'd heard a moment ago, and also by the look of consternation now on the miss's lovely countenance) that she had most likely sent Penelope's sculpture of a half-clad Aphrodite toppling to the floor.

Being something of an artist, and having dabbled in sculpting a time or two, Blackwood had found the statue to be woefully lacking in symmetry; he marveled that the piece had remained erect this long. Good riddance to the thing, he thought to himself.

And then he settled down in the mist-shrouded waters, allowing himself a long moment to admire the perfect symmetry of the beauty moving ever nearer to the pool. With such a vision of loveliness in the flesh, who had need of some bulky Aphrodite sculpture? Indeed, Miss Mirabella Lavinia Darlington could doubtless cast a thousand Aphrodites in the shade.

She still wore her riding habit, but the form-fitting velvet did little to conceal her generous curves, which could cause a monk to forsake his heavenly vows. God, but she was Beauty's self. He wondered at the fact that Diana had not once set his heart to strumming so wildly as the sight of this woman did now. Indeed, he was surprised that he could not, for the life of him, even conjure up a mental image of the woman he had once thought he loved so much. It appeared that Miss Mirabella Darlington held the power to cause all his memories of Diana to become so much vapor.

Imagine that.

Diana had loved another more than he. Though that fact had recently haunted him, had turned his heart to ice for far too long, he suddenly felt the ice begin to thaw.

Spring had finally come to his embittered soul.

And that spring, amazingly enough, bore the name, the face, the body, the refreshing spirit of one Mirabella Lavinia Darlington.

At long last, Diana's—and, yes, Matthew's—

final deceit could no longer rip Blackwood's soul asunder. He had found a balm. He had, he thought, thanking the stars, the heavens—even God, who had once seemed to have turned His back to him—met the Unmatchable Miss Mirabella.

Mirabella, having bashed a toe against a statue of Aphrodite in the entranceway (a statue that had not been there the last time she'd entered the bathhouse, long ago, a statue that was now lying prone on the floor) cursed silently. Leave it to her godmama to decide to redecorate and not mention the fact! And wasn't it just like Penelope to commission a statue that was far too large, too outlandish—and damn it all—deucedly easy to topple, and have it placed in such an inconvenient spot!

But of course, Mirabella had other matters to worry about. She'd come to the spa in hopes of finding her spaniel but, while tiptoeing round the place, had heard a soft purr that could only belong to Sasha. Following the sounds, she'd entered the bathhouse and had, dash it all, run smack-dab into that blasted statue. Pity her toe had broken off an alarming amount of Aphrodite's hems ... and pity, too, that she'd gone and stoved her toe (while trying not to fall face-first over the downed statue!) on a part of the goddess's anatomy that had doubtless caused many a mythical god to drool.

Mirabella quickly dismissed the discomfort of her toe and hobbled into the pool area. Steam obscured her view, and the pungent smell of the mineral waters assailed her nostrils.

"Sasha?" she called. "If you are here, you busy hunter, then you'd best show yourself! I am not at all pleased with you. Imagine, devouring a defenseless spaniel!"

There came no sound of Sasha's mewlings. There did, however, come the rich timbre of a man's voice.

"Do not tell me you are in search of yet another four-footed companion," came a disembodied voice that echoed over the water.

Mirabella started.

"Who's there?" she demanded—though, in truth, she could well imagine who she'd intruded upon.

There came the sound of swishing water, and then, beside the fount where the waters of the hot spring gushed forth, she detected a handsome face. The face belonged to none other than the Earl of Blackwood.

"I thought you'd gone back to Stormhaven to await Lord Warwick," he said.

The rich rumble of his voice caused a tingle of sensation to ripple up Mirabella's spine. She strove to regain her composure, but such a thing proved to be a difficult task indeed. She couldn't help but wonder if he was fully dressed in the pool—and the man's voice did odd things to her senses. "You are wrong," she said. "I didn't go in search of Lord Warwick at all."

"I'm glad to hear that," he replied, flashing her a bright grin.

Mirabella was momentarily taken back—both by his words and because her mind all too readily conjured up a detailed image of what she might see should his lordship step out of the pool.

She felt her cheeks turn scarlet and marveled at the wantonness of her imagination. Surely she should turn and take leave of the man; any young lady with refined sensibilities would not linger a moment longer given the situation.

The Unmatchable Miss Mirabella 125

"Forgive me, my lord," said Mirabella quickly. "I did not mean to intrude." She made a motion to leave.

Blackwood's voice, echoing across the distance between them, stilled her movements. "You needn't hurry off, Miss Darlington."

Oh, but I do, Mirabella said to herself, her back now turned toward him. She thought of Blackwood in the pool, no doubt naked. She thought (scandalously enough!) of his lean and muscled form being bathed by the waters. She must leave. This wasn't at all proper. He already believed her to be a reckless flirt, too much like his departed Lady Diana.

Mirabella frowned. Why did it bother her that Blackwood had once been in love, had plighted his troth to another? And why should she care if he thought her to be too much like the woman who had claimed to love him in return and then had deceived him?

"I must go," Mirabella said. "I am searching for the spaniel I purchased, and a—another pet I seem to have, er, misplaced."

"Ah, so the tiger is yours. I should have guessed."

Unable to help herself, Mirabella chanced a peek at him over one shoulder. "You have *seen* Sasha, my lord?" she asked, the barest hint of hope in her voice. Through the whispering mists, she perceived his nod of affirmation. "Where? When?"

"You are but a moment too late, Miss Darlington." Blackwood motioned toward the marble columns facing Stormhaven. "The beast you seek went that way. Made off with my best rosewood cane as well."

"Oh, dear. I shall replace the cane, my lord."

"No need."

"I insist."

"And I," he said, the sound of his voice low, intoxicating, "insist that you do not. Your tiger seemed happy gnawing on the thing. Better to have him—or is Sasha a she?—devouring canes rather than spaniels, I think."

Mirabella was surprised at the smile she felt curving her lips. "Sasha is a she, my lord. And yes, I quite agree with you; I would much rather she occupied herself with a cane and not another spaniel."

Blackwood flashed her a grin, one that nearly lit the spa. "You are certain Sasha is a she?"

He was teasing her, Mirabella knew. "I am quite certain, my lord," she answered. "Though I made a grave error in choosing a pup of the wrong gender for the duchess, I did make a point of knowing whether Sasha was male or female. You see," she added, her own voice taking on a teasing note, "I've heard tell that male tigers can be frightfully full of themselves."

"And you'll suffer none of that, eh?"

"Not where tigers are concerned. Good day, my lord." Mirabella moved away, but made it only as far as the middle of the archway before Blackwood spoke again, his voice low and throbbing.

"And what about where men are concerned, Miss Darlington? Have you always shied away from dominating male figures?"

Mirabella stood poised beneath the archway, her back toward Blackwood. She lifted her chin, staring at nothing, feeling the heat of his gaze on her. "I do not believe, my lord, that I have ever shied away from anyone or anything."

"But you are doing it now."

"Excuse me?"

He laughed softly, the sound echoing all around. "You heard me aright, Miss Darlington. Pray, do not pretend otherwise. What I am asking is why are you always in such a blasted hurry to relieve yourself of my company?"

Mirabella's stomach whirled with butterflies as the husky sound of his voice penetrated her very being. "You are being ridiculous, my lord."

"Am I? 'Tis obvious you are biting at the bit to leave."

"I—I told you, I am searching for Sasha."

"Your tiger is no doubt a mile away by now."

"That may be true, my lord," Mirabella grudgingly agreed, "but even if I were not looking for the animal, it—would hardly be proper for me to linger here while you ... while you partake of the waters."

"Perhaps to some people it would be unseemly, but not to you, I wager."

"And what do you mean by that, my lord?" she asked, pivoting round.

" 'Twas but a compliment, I assure you. I meant only that you are truly a free spirit." He grinned at her. "I am glad you turned about—for a moment, I feared you'd become timid."

Mirabella studiously ignored his disarming smile. "I have never been called timid, my lord."

"Good. Then I trust you'll not be attempting to dart quickly away." Blackwood pushed his arms through the water, creating ripples atop the bubbling, misty pool. "Have you ever taken the cure of your godmama's spa, Miss Darlington?"

Mirabella wondered why he seemed bent on prolonging their conversation. She thought of saying good-bye, but curiosity got the best of her. And since the outline of his body beneath the waters was hidden in mist and bubbles, she decided there could be little harm in remaining a moment longer.

"I've done so a time or two in the past," Mirabella told him. And perhaps hoping to shock him a little, she added, "I've also enjoyed many an *onsen* in the Far East, my lord."

He cocked one dark brow at her. "Ah, nothing so tame as the hot springs in Bath for you, eh?"

Mirabella shook her head. "Once one has plunged oneself into a blood-red *ofuro* scented with hibiscus, there is nothing to compare. Even now, I can recall the chattering of monkeys in the trees nearby . . . the lovely scent and taste of the waters."

"You did not speak of the *ofuro*, the baths, at dinner last night. Pity, that. I should like to hear more about your adventures in the Far East, Miss Darlington. Perhaps we could compare observations."

"You have traveled there, my lord?" she asked, surprised.

"Once. Years ago . . . a lifetime ago, it seems now. The *onsen*, the hot spring, I found was in a snowfield, the waters milky-white. I remember lying down and watching as the melting icicles dripped down to nothingness . . ."

"And did you, my lord, discover your inner soul there?" Mirabella asked quietly, recalling the moment in which she had almost done just that.

"Alas, no," Blackwood said, his dark gaze searing into hers across the distance. "I was but a young buck enjoying my Grand Tour. I hadn't the patience for such a potentially dangerous venture. Now, however, I would very much like to visit the *onsen* again. I'll gladly leave Bath to the supposedly proper ladies and gentlemen who seek nothing more than their seasonal suitors and gravitate toward the dying searching for a miracle, and the restless seeking a new love." The mesmerizing color of his black eyes deepened as he added, "Perhaps in the near future I will find a traveling companion who is unafraid to search for the inner soul, to plunge into a blood-red *ofuro*, and to discern beauty in the distant screech of the monkeys."

Mirabella, hypnotized by his words, gave herself a sudden mental shake. "I—I hope you do, my lord. Now, if you'll excuse me, I really must be going."

He let out a sigh. "There you go again, becoming timid with me."

"Hardly that, my lord!"

"Who'd have thought?" Blackwood said, as though he hadn't heard her. "This timid streak in you is not at all in keeping with the Unmatchable Miss Mirabella I've heard so much about."

Mirabella stiffened, feeling her face flush. "Oh, how I loathe that label affixed to me! I am hardly 'unmatchable'!"

"Faith," he murmured, almost chattily, "you are quick to anger."

"And you, sir, forever manage to be insufferable!"

"Forgive me. I don't mean to be. I suppose it is because I've never encountered anyone quite like you."

"Or mayhap you have been too long gone from society," she said, bothered that he obviously thought she was odd.

"*Touché*," Blackwood whispered, smiling. Sitting in the middle of the pool, he looked for all the world like a Roman gladiator come to life, with his wet hair plastered to his head and a lone lock curling down across his high forehead. The mere sight of him caused her blood to surge through her veins with mind-spinning speed.

"I must admit, Miss Darlington," Blackwood continued, perhaps unaware of what the sight of him did to her, "that when I first met you I was reminded of someone I once knew. This lady, too, was Beauty itself ... but she proved to be rash and reckless, unmindful of what havoc her charms could wreak on the gentlemen she encountered."

Mirabella held perfectly still, listening and noting above all else the pain that crept into Blackwood's black eyes.

"I fell in love with the lady—or rather, I believed I was in love with her," he said.

Something in Mirabella softened, pushed past the anger. Mayhap in his own way, he was trying to reach out to someone, to talk of the pain he felt. It would be cruel of her to take her leave of him now—and in truth, she did not want to go. Not yet.

"And then, my lord?" she asked gently. "What happened?"

Blackwood gave a rueful laugh, staring into the shadows of the spa. "I rode off into battle with the naive illusion of every untried soldier—that war would be glorious or dashing or even easy. It was none of those things, I assure you. War is filled with horror and ineptness. Its triumphs are laced with terror, and the long and lonely nights are filled with the groans of the dying and the frantic prayers of the living.

"I returned to England with a ball of lead in my thigh, the remembered screams of my dead comrades ringing in my ears, the taste of French soil on the back of my tongue, and the foolish thought that if only I could reach home, I would feel right again. I thought that once I saw my brother, my betrothed, my *home*, all would be well. How wrong I was. I found my brother and my fiancée dead and lying in state. And my home ... well, that proved to be as foreign to me as the battlefield of Waterloo had first been."

"I am sorry," Mirabella whispered.

Blackwood returned his gaze to hers. "It isn't your pity I seek," he murmured.

Mirabella did not flinch beneath the searing heat of his intense eyes. "It isn't pity that I feel for you, my lord, but rather a kinship. I—I too have lost someone very dear to me, and I, too, once thought that if I came home, back to Stormhaven, my mourning would find an end ..."'

"But it hasn't," Blackwood guessed.

Mirabella shook her head. "Not totally," she admitted.

"Tell me about it, if you wish," he said, his soft voice filled with a sweetness Mirabella had heretofore believed him incapable of demonstrating.

It was that very sweetness that scaled the invisible wall she had built round her heart since her father's death. Suddenly she found herself talking of the very thing she'd been trying to forget.

"My father died in a carriage accident little more than a year ago, my lord," she began, the words pouring out of her. "He'd been hero, mentor, father, and mother to me, ever encouraging me to be independent and original. But then, suddenly, he was gone, and I found myself an heiress, thrust into an arena I'd been avoiding all my life. You cannot imagine all the fortune hunters who pushed their way into my path.

"I hated that they sought my hand—or rather my inheritance—when I was still mourning my father's passing. I found the only way to deal with the onslaught of suitors was to indulge in my originality, to blaze my own trail in life, so to speak, and to take myself out of Town as quickly as possible. But there were those who followed me even into the wilds of Bengal ... and I fear that my recklessness only encouraged these gentlemen, as well as a sultan, and even a Turkish slave, to offer for my hand."

" 'Tis no wonder you believe males can be frightfully full of themselves," Blackwood murmured. "So you thought to thwart these suitors by becoming even more free-spirited, even more reckless, and in flirting with not one man but many?"

Mirabella stiffened. "I am nothing like Lady Diana, my lord."

"Tell me, Miss Darlington, are you always so direct?"

"When it suits me, yes. As I told you, I never back away from anyone or anything."

A thick silence welled between them before Blackwood asked, "Did you meet with Warwick after we parted company in the field earlier today?"

His question took Mirabella by surprise. "Now who is being direct, my lord?"

"Did you meet with Warwick?" he pressed.

"Does it matter?"

"Yes," he said simply. "It does."

Mirabella felt the force of his words all the way to her toes. He was obviously hoping she *hadn't* met with the man. But she *had* met with Warwick, and she found she could not lie.

"I . . . as a matter of fact, I did speak with Lord Monty today."

Blackwood's stark smile vanished. "I see."

"No, I don't believe you do, sir. Lord Warwick and I did not go riding, if that is what you are thinking. Instead, we talked. Briefly." Quietly, she added, "We spoke of you."

"Me." Blackwood was not surprised—and obviously none too happy. "I can only imagine what rot Warwick told you. Faith," he muttered, "I've no doubt but the cad heaped insult upon my name."

"On the contrary, my lord, his words were actually kind."

Blackwood laughed in disbelief.

" 'Tis true," Mirabella insisted. "Lord Monty

said you are an honest man who does not deserve the pain you've been dealt in life. He—he said he wished things could have turned out differently between you two."

Blackwood frowned. "Monty always did have a way with words when a beautiful woman was involved."

Mirabella ignored him, saying, "Lord Warwick wished me well concerning our, uh, supposed betrothal, and then he departed for Town."

Blackwood clearly had trouble digesting this information. "Monty is gone? Just like that? I can hardly believe it!"

"It would seem, my lord, that your plan of thwarting his pursuit of me worked famously."

"And doubtless you are angry and damn me for spinning such a tall tale about the two of us being betrothed. Monty may very well spread the word about Town."

"I *am* angry," Mirabella admitted. "But I do not damn you. Never that. And I would never intentionally deceive you." She would *not* allow him to continue thinking she was anything like Lady Diana. Mirabella was quite unlike his deceased betrothed, and for some inexplicable reason, it was important to her that he realize this.

For a moment, there was nothing but the splashing of water from the fount and the electrified, mist-filled air between them.

Finally, Blackwood spoke into the silence. "Then you are one of the few who does not condemn me, Miss Darlington. I'll be the first to admit I have been a bit of a stuffed shirt of late, an ogre even. I would have been blind not to have noticed how the Duchess of Ravenscar and her friends cornered you at the party last night. No doubt they filled your head with stories of how I've been a brute. There was a time when that realization would have sent me into a further state of agitation. But not now."

"Oh?" Mirabella murmured, almost hesitantly.

"Indeed. You see, it has suddenly occurred to me that the past is the past . . . and tomorrow—ah, tomorrow is staring me in the face. I would do well to meet it head on."

So saying, Blackwood glided away from the fountain and made a motion to stand upright. Mirabella's heart fluttered rapidly. Good Lord, he thought to arise from the waters, with not a stitch of clothing with which to cover himself!

She instantly whirled away, blushing, and wondered what in the devil she'd gotten herself into.

11

Blackwood moved to the side of the pool and hoisted himself out of the waters. He caught a glimpse of Mirabella's retreating back.

"Don't leave," he called, his voice husky.

She halted her steps and turned partly toward him, trembling slightly, imagining him naked and dripping. "I—I didn't mean to intrude, my lord. I . . ." She paused, raising her eyes only enough to see the water puddling around his bare feet, falling from his breeches-clad legs. "You're dressed!" she gasped.

Blackwood grinned. "But of course."

She whirled to fully face him. "You actually jumped into the spa fully clothed? *You*, a man who is such a stickler for convention?"

" 'Tis true," he said, "though even I can hardly explain it. I was not at all pleased with the way in which we parted company earlier."

"So you came to the spa and just threw yourself—fully clothed—into the water?"

"Something like that," he admitted. "I fear your free-spirited ways are already influencing my behavior."

She obviously did not believe him, for she glared daggers at him. "Oh, what a perfect fool I have made of myself! I have been standing here, worrying about how to react to your . . . your state of undress, and now I find that you are not undressed at all!"

"You would rather I was undressed?"

Her cheeks flamed. "Of course not, my lord!"

"Please, call me Christian." He flashed her a grin. "And if you do not mind, I would like very much to call you Bella."

She hesitated, not quite knowing how to react to his sudden affability. "I—I think I should be going, my lor—"

"Christian," he said. "And must you go so soon?"

"Yes, I must. It is highly improper of me to be here, my lor—Christian."

"And since when have you ever worried about impropriety?" he asked.

Mirabella lifted her chin. "Since I met you," she said matter-of-factly. And then, before he could stop her, she darted out of the spa.

A grin lifted the corners of his mouth. The day that had begun so wretchedly was ending on a high note.

Whistling and still dripping, Blackwood gathered up his coat and shoes and socks and left the spa. He made his way down the hill to the guest house below, allowing himself to conjure up images of the Unmatchable Miss Mirabella.

Unmatchable, eh? He did not think so. It was his opinion that Bella simply had not had the good fortune to meet the man with whom she was destined to share the rest of her life—until now, that is.

Blackwood happily quickened his pace. For the first time since Waterloo, his leg felt right as rain, and his heart ... ah, his heart was filling with the sweetness of love.

Mirabella slept restlessly. Her dreams were haunted by visions of the handsome Blackwood.

Lord, would her thoughts never be free of the man?

But there was the rub; his lordship *wasn't* pursuing her. He hadn't recited so much as one poem in her presence, hadn't toasted her eyelashes, or even sent any pretty phrases her way.

So why was she so obsessed with the man? No doubt he considered her a perfectly odd creature, what with her outlandish mode of dress and her habit of constantly misplacing her animals. Too, at five-and-twenty Mirabella knew she was considered long on the shelf. She was sensible enough to realize it was only the size of her vast inheritance and mayhap her personal charms that prompted the many bucks even to glance in her direction.

But Blackwood had no need of a fortune, and he seemed content with his solitude. He did not appear to have marriage on his mind—nor did she, she told herself.

So why the deuce was she *dreaming* about the man? Zeus and Minerva, but one might think she was a ninnyhammer who had turned hopelessly rhapsodic over a man she hardly knew!

She punched her feather-filled pillow, and tried yet again to clear her head and fall asleep. She managed only a few hours of light slumber. The other hours were filled with dreams of a dark-eyed man whose arms enfolded her and whose kisses were passionate ...

"Lawks, Miss Bella! Are you thinkin' t' sleep the day away? Lord, yer worse than that swoonin' duchess who sleeps t' noon! If you don't soon open yer eyes and greet the day, you'll miss yer picnic with Lord What's-'is'-name!"

Mirabella opened one bleary eye as Annie bustled about the bedchamber. She whipped open the curtains, opened a window to let in an earthy-smelling breeze, and then hurried to Mirabella's wardrobe to help her choose a gown.

Mirabella's sluggish brain began to spin.

"Good Lord, Annie, must you move so fast? The house isn't ablaze, is it? What time is it, anyway?"

"It be half past eleven. Time t' get yer lazy bones out o' bed, Miss Bella! Lord What's-'is'-name is even now pacin' a hole in yer godmama's fine carpet in the front drawin' room. He be sweatin' already, too. Moppin' at 'is brow, 'e is, and you 'aven' even shown yer face! I be thinkin' yer in for a *long* picnic, Miss Bella."

Mirabella groaned. Why in the devil had she agreed to join Lord Robertshaw for a picnic? With the way her luck was running, his lordship had most likely had a team hitched up to one of the many carriages in Nellie's stables, and was doubtlessly planning to guide the team to some faraway location where he could be alone with her.

Blast!

Mirabella tossed off the bedclothes and propped herself up on her elbows. Annie seemed to be in high spirits this morning.

"Which gown today, Miss Bella?" she asked. "They all be quite fetchin'."

"I don't know that I want to appear *too* fetching in Lord Robertshaw's eyes, Annie."

"Sure you do, Miss Bella! A man is a man, even if you don't wish t' capture 'is interest."

Mirabella sighed. She had no intention of encouraging Lord Robertshaw. She climbed out of bed and moved into the antechamber to begin her toilette, saying over one shoulder, "Annie, you'd best find something suitable to wear as well. You'll be joining us."

"Oh, Miss Bella! Don't say that I'm t' be yer chaperone!"

"That is precisely what I am saying," Mirabella

replied. "You did not think I would suffer through a picnic alone with him, did you?"

She had to smother a giggle when she heard Annie's muttered protest. Obviously, the young maid was not at all pleased to have to spend time away from her handsome new friend Haluk.

Mirabella descended the stairs at precisely noon. Much to her delight, Annie had chosen a stylishly embroidered muslin gown for her with a soft shawl as outerwear. The outfit was completed with a comely bonnet adorned with forget-me-nots.

Mirabella carried a tall stick parasol in her gloved hands and headed for the front drawing room where Lord Robertshaw waited. Annie followed.

"Miss Darlington!" cried Lord Robertshaw. "What a vision you present this day!" He gave a gallant bow, then reached for her hand and pressed a kiss to the back, all the while gazing up at her with puppy-like eyes.

Mirabella gently extricated her hand from his overly tight hold. "Lord Robertshaw."

"Our carriage awaits us, Miss Darlington. Cook has prepared a lovely lunch, and your godmama was ever so kind in suggesting I drive you out to a grassy knoll nearby that is complete with a babbling stream and a grand view of the surrounding area."

"Famous," said Mirabella, making a mental note to scold Aunt Nellie for having given such advice.

They remained within the drawing room for a few minutes longer—time enough for his lordship to toss some pretty phrases her way—and then headed outside for the carriage.

Lord Robertshaw had chosen a curricle and dispensed with the use of a groom. Annie seated herself on the perch behind them, as Mirabella, beside Lord Robertshaw, tried to get comfortable in the small vehicle.

She'd no sooner settled herself than his lordship sent the team leaping forward. Annie gasped. Mirabella clutched her bonnet lest it be blown away, and grabbed tight to the seat lest she be toppled overboard.

Busy trying to handle the reins of Nellie's spirited cattle, Lord Robertshaw was unable to utter an apology. They twice came to a a jarring halt while his lordship inexpertly attempted to let the horses know that he was in charge of them.

Mirabella considered taking over the reins, then quickly dismissed the notion. She had no mind to embarrass his lordship. She would as soon suffer the delay than make him uncomfortable. Though the young buck was proving frightfully wet behind the ears, he did seem to have a good heart.

"Forgive me, Miss Darlington," he begged, sweating profusely, "I can't seem to get ... the beasts to ... move in the right ... direction!"

"Perhaps you are holding the reins too tightly, my lord," suggested Mirabella.

He tried a lighter touch, and the horses responded nimbly.

"Fancy that!" he cried.

"Yes," said Mirabella. "Fancy that."

Overjoyed by this turn of events, Lord Robertshaw soon set the horses to a fast pace. The carriage careened down the rough country road, nearly upsetting both Mirabella and Annie from their seats. Mirabella soon feared for their lives!

When the carriage reached the top of a long and steep hill, and the horses made motion to charge down the other side, Mirabella decided enough was enough. A sweating Lord Robertshaw was looking decidedly pop-eyed—he was clearly terrified—and the horses were straining to be freed from the untrained hands guiding them.

"Pray, allow me," said Mirabella, quickly taking the reins from his hands.

She allowed the confused beasts a moment to adjust to her lead, then steered them off to the side of the road where they came to a halt.

Lord Robertshaw looked like a pup who had been kicked in the backside.

Hoping to soothe his bruised pride, Mirabella said, "I fear my godmama's cattle can be temperamental at times, my lord."

Lord Robertshaw seemed happy to overlook his own inexperience. "Shall we head for the stream?" he suggested.

She nodded. The sooner this picnic began the sooner it would be finished.

One disaster led to another. His lordship slipped a heel while trying to maneuver himself, the basket, and Mirabella along a winding path. He was reduced to hobbling along, trying to act as though nothing was amiss. Mirabella wished he would cast off his insufferable boots, but, alas, he did not.

He stumbled while leading Mirabella over a small footbridge. The basket went tumbling. Mirabella nearly lost her own footing. And his lordship, much to his obvious chagrin, found himself on his knees, clinging to the side of the bridge.

"Good 'eavens!" muttered Annie from behind them.

Mirabella helped the gentleman to his feet, noted his tight frown, and took a step back. "I fear this bridge is uneven, my lord. I can only imagine how many others have tripped over its boards."

Lord Robertshaw agreed with her. He quickly bent to scoop up the roasted fowl, hunks of cheese, and loaf of bread that had toppled out of the basket, and then led the way to the other side.

The outing did not improve after that. His lordship, trying to be gallant and stooping to pick a bloom for Mirabella, got stung by a bee.

"Ow!" he cried.

Annie smothered a giggle.

His right hand soon swelled to the size of a melon.

Mirabella, trying to be helpful, hurried down the bank to the stream and soaked a linen napkin in the cool water. She motioned for Lord Robertshaw to come stand beside her so she could place the waterlogged linen against his bee sting.

His lordship, however, seemed to have recovered sufficiently to turn his thoughts to romance. He shot down the bank and knelt before her atop a soft mound of dirt.

"I—I do believe I have fallen in love with you, Miss Darlington!" he exclaimed.

Mirabella frowned. Not another proposal!

Would this afternoon ever end?

Blackwood awoke that morning with a strong urge to seek out Mirabella and apologize for his roguish behavior.

He strode down the knoll to Penelope's house, but learned Bella had gone out. After Penelope told him that Bella had gone off with Lord Robertshaw for a picnic, he soon departed as well.

He knew a keen jealousy at the thought of Mirabella entertaining young Lord Robertshaw. Blackwood did not doubt but that Robertshaw would make a play for Bella's attentions. He frowned. He'd ventured down to the main house in hopes of taking a walk with Bella. He'd even brought his charcoals and sketch pad.

In a protective mood, he saddled one of Penelope's fastest horses and made haste toward the knoll where, according to Penelope, Robertshaw had taken Bella.

He did not give a thought to his healing thigh (which felt a world better since last evening's dip in the spa), nor did he consider the possibility that Mirabella might not welcome being saved from Lord Robertshaw's attentions.

All he knew was that he needed to see for himself that she was not cast into any kind of uncomfortable situation. She was a free spirit. And free spirits needed a free rein.

Mirabella, standing near the stream and gazing down at Lord Robertshaw, considered how she might best extricate herself from this predicament.

While she was choosing her words, Lord Robertshaw began to twitch. First his bended knee began to jerk, then his midsection, and then his upper body. Before long, he was quivering all over.

Mirabella looked closer . . . and soon puzzled out the cause of his distress. He had thrown himself onto bended knee atop an anthill!

"Excuse me, my lord," she said, interrupting yet another long speech describing his love for her, "but you seem to have ants crawling all over you."

"Ants?"

His lordship let out a pathetic howl. He jumped to his feet, hopped about for a moment or two, and then threw himself belly-first into the fast-rushing stream. His eyes bulged and his mouth hung open. He thrashed about in the stream, slapping his limbs up and down. "Ants!" he cried. "I *detest* ants!"

Mirabella smothered a giggle; the sight of him flapping about in the stream was that absurd.

"Surely, my lord," she said, "you must have realized that all picnics come complete with ants."

"*This* many?" he cried.

"Perhaps you should not have knelt atop their home."

"Good God," he moaned. "What a mess I have made of the moment!"

He shot up out of the stream, then began to splash back toward Mirabella. He sloshed up onto the bank, took her by the shoulders, and declared, "I had hoped to offer you my hand in marriage, Miss Darlington!" His brown eyes were filled with the youthful exuberance of first love. "I do hope you will accept my offer!"

He bussed her on the cheek, a wet and sloppy kiss that left much to be desired.

Mirabella, trying to dodge the kiss, placed her hands against his chest and attempted gently to push him away.

But Lord Robertshaw proved to be more ardent than she had anticipated.

"No," he said passionately. "Do not deny me. I know you will soon love me as I love you. I know we shall be happy together!"

"My lord!" Mirabella gasped. "This is most improper! Pray, release me this instant!"

"I cannot! I doubt I shall ever be able to let you go."

Mirabella panicked as he crushed her to his chest.

She was debating whether she should push him back into the stream or just slap him soundly when there came a sound of charging hoofbeats.

"Coo, Miss Bella!" cried Annie. " 'Tis that 'andsome Lord Blackwood! 'E be comin' t' save you from Lord What's-'is-name!"

Both Robertshaw and Mirabella looked up.

Lord Blackwood, astride one of Penelope's finest

horses, came to a halt before them, beneath the spreading limbs of an elm tree.

"I suggest, Lord Robertshaw, that you release the lady," he said. "Obviously, she is not of the mind to endure your youthful pawing."

"Blackwood!" gulped Robertshaw, staring up at him.

Blackwood slid from the saddle, secured his horse's reins to a tree branch, and moved down the bank. There was no hint of lameness in his gait. Indeed, he appeared fit enough to give the young buck exactly what he deserved.

"Tell me, Lord Robertshaw," he demanded, "what is it about the fair Miss Darlington that captures your interest? Is it the sound of her melodic voice? Her bold spirit? Her beauty?"

"'T-tis all of those things!" claimed Lord Robertshaw.

"I see," said Blackwood, clearly skeptical. He backed the young lord into the stream.

Out of earshot of Mirabella, Blackwood said, "I don't suppose it is the lady's fortune you are after. Tell me it isn't."

The younger lord, quaking in his soggy boots, said nothing.

Blackwood eyed the man, a dangerous glint of warning in his black gaze. "If you know what's best, Robertshaw, you'll leave. Now."

Robertshaw did not need to be told twice. He scurried out of the stream, gave an embarrassed nod toward Mirabella, and darted away, heading for the curricle.

Annie clapped her hands in glee. "Good riddance t' 'im, I say!"

Mirabella frowned, glaring at Blackwood. "That was hardly necessary, my lord."

"I disagree. In my opinion I came a moment too late."

Mirabella lifted her chin. "I had things well in hand, my lord."

"Christian."

"What?"

Blackwood smiled. "You are to call me Christian—or have you forgotten yesterday, Bella?"

Annie's eyes lit up with sudden interest. "Yesterday?" she asked. "Coo, Miss Bella, what 'appened yesterday?"

Mirabella felt herself blush. "Hush, Annie," she ordered. To Blackwood, she said, "You are trying to change the subject, my lor—Christian."

His smile deepened. "I am at that," he admitted. "I grow weary speaking of young Robertshaw. The buck isn't worthy of your attention."

"Pray, allow me to decide whom I should or should not see."

"I will—as long as it *isn't* Robertshaw—or Warwick."

Mirabella tried to summon up anger toward him, but found she could not. His smile was too endearing, warm and plainly heartfelt. And, she conceded, he had come to her rescue.

Blackwood watched her frown disappear. "I am forgiven, then?"

Mirabella smiled. "Yes ... I suppose so." She paused. "But there is one problem."

"What's that?"

"Lord Robertshaw has taken the curricle. Annie and I shall be forced to walk back to Stormhaven."

"Ah, I see. Well then, I suppose I can do naught but offer to walk with you—for protection, of course."

"Protection?"

He nodded, moving up the bank toward her. "I hear," he said, dropping his voice to a whisper, "there is a tiger loose in the Cotswolds."

Mirabella feigned a gasp. "No! Truly? Well, I daresay my maid and I shall have need of your presence. Do join us, please."

He gave her a low bow, righted himself, and said, "Anything for a damsel in distress." His eyes lit with merriment at this deliberate reminder of that moment in the tent at the fair.

"Ah," said Mirabella, her heart feeling light as a feather, "always the gentleman, aren't you?"

"I try to be," he said softly, his gaze warming. "Shall we be going, then?"

He shook his head, a lock of hair falling romantically over his brow. "Not yet."

Mirabella gave him a puzzled look. "I don't understand."

" 'Tis simple. This business of dashing to your rescue has left me famished, Bella. What do you say we share the picnic young Robertshaw has had packed?"

"I would say," replied Mirabella, "that Lord Robertshaw would be highly insulted."

Blackwood feigned a shudder. "Well, we wouldn't want that—or would we?"

Mirabella pretended to consider the matter, then, dissolving into laughter, said, "I do believe it would be a shame to let the food go to waste."

He gave her a conspiratorial wink. "My thoughts exactly!"

He offered her his arm, and Mirabella, seeing that Annie had already unpacked the picnic and spread it nearby, placed her gloved hand in the warm crook of his arm.

Together, they strolled the rest of the way up the grassy bank.

Annie, seeing their approach, cooed with delight. "Lawks, Miss Bella, does this mean I don't 'ave t' play yer chaperone now? It be my opinion—beggin' yer pardon, o' course—that yer a bit old t' 'ave need of a chaperone. Too, you ain't in London now, but in the country. We don't fuss with such stuffiness 'ere. And do be truthful now, Miss Bella, but you never did fuss about such things afore."

"Annie!" Mirabella said, blushing crimson. "You shall remain here with me."

Blackwood, however, leaned closer to Mirabella and said, "What a breath of fresh air she is. And look, Bella, she has already uncorked the champagne. Shall we indulge?"

Mirabella found she could not deny the man.

12

Mirabella could not remember ever spending such a pleasant afternoon as the one she shared with Blackwood. In spite of his earlier intimidating manner, he proved to be quite entertaining. Indeed, it was difficult for her to even imagine that his lordship had so recently chosen to hibernate within Penelope's guest house.

They soon consumed both the champagne and the food. After they had all helped to pack the remains of the picnic into the hamper, they set off across the meadows that would lead them back to Stormhaven.

The walk back home took the rest of the afternoon, but none of them minded. The rolling countryside opened up before them. Rambling hedges and fences of honey-colored stone laced the sprawling meadows, and every so often there could be seen a charming swing gate or two. In the distance, built along a winding stream, was a cluster of quaint, low stone cottages, the gardens of which were ablaze with roses.

Mirabella marveled at the view. *I have truly come home*, she thought, taking in the splendor. And though she'd so recently felt saddened at the thought of treading this countryside without her father, she no longer experienced such pangs. Instead, she felt healed.

She glanced over at Blackwood, who walked beside her. 'Twas his presence, she knew, that caused her heart to feel light, her soul carefree.

As they were walking along a small footpath that led through a swing gate, Blackwood suggested they all pause and enjoy the scenery. He tethered the horse's reins to the gate latch.

He removed a sketch pad and charcoals from within a leather packet fastened to his mount's saddle, and motioning for Mirabella to sit beside him on the low stone wall, he began to sketch a spreading hawthorn tree that stood in solitary splendor in a meadow.

Mirabella could not help but admire the way in which his hand moved with such ease over the pad. Soon, they were discussing lines and shadings and the play of light over the fields.

Annie, bored, wandered off to pluck some wildflowers with which to make a bouquet. Neither Mirabella nor Blackwood noted her absence; they were far too engrossed in the sketching ... and each other.

Blackwood suggested that Mirabella turn her own hand to the sketch. Delighted, she eagerly took the pad and charcoals he passed to her. She found, however, that she couldn't quite capture the precise bend of one of the tree's limbs.

"Ah," said Blackwood, "perhaps if you bring the line down, just a tad. Like this." His hand covered hers as he helped to guide the charcoal.

Suddenly, Mirabella found she wasn't thinking of the hawthorn but of Blackwood's touch. 'Twas warm, soft, and gentle ... just like the man. Wondrous sensations coursed up her arm to swirl through her body in a shower of heady sparks. Was he, too, feeling the same longing that pounded within her breast?

She chanced a glance up at him and she was both startled and pleased to see that he was gazing intently at her. She could lose herself in the depths of those black eyes, she thought. Indeed, should he take her into his arms, she would be able to deny him nothing.

Her heart tripped a beat as Blackwood leaned slightly toward her. Was he going to kiss her? She very much hoped he would. Of their own accord her lips parted, her lashes fluttered downward. Her heart strumming wildly, she waited for the instant when he would claim her mouth with his.

She waited in vain. Annie's screech of alarm shattered the moment.

Mirabella snapped her eyes open, and both she and Blackwood trained their sights on the young maid. Annie stood in the middle of the field, jumping up and down and waving her arms.

"Yer tiger, Miss Bella!" she cried. " 'E be near, I swear! Oh, do hurry! I fear that beast is lookin' for yer godmama's sheep!"

Mirabella jumped to her feet, momentarily forgetting the sketch pad and charcoals, which tumbled to the ground.

"I *am* sorry," she said. She quickly bent to retrieve them at precisely the same moment as Blackwood. They bumped heads.

Mirabella pulled back, mortified. What a perfect ninnyhammer she must seem to him! And what must he think of her, now that she'd all but puckered her lips for a kiss he might—or might not—have intended? It did not bear contemplating.

"You are not hurt, are you, Bella?"

Only my pride, she thought, lowering her head to hide her shame. "No. I—I am fine." She hurriedly tried to collect the charcoals, but managed only to smear the stuff on her hands. Tears of frustration threatened to overwhelm her.

"Leave them," he said. He cupped one hand about her elbow and gently helped her to her feet.

"For now, let us try and locate that tiger of yours, shall we?"

She managed a nod before she turned away and headed toward Annie. She only hoped Blackwood hadn't noticed the wetness in her eyes; she'd embarrassed herself enough for one day.

Blackwood watched Mirabella hurry toward the maid. He'd seen the shimmer of tears in her lovely eyes—and knew he was the cause of them.

What a fool he'd been just now! He cursed himself soundly for not kissing her when he'd had the chance. Her softly parted lips had beckoned to him certainly, but he was ever mindful that he must tread carefully where Mirabella was concerned. He did not wish to appear an overeager, lusty lord; she had known too many of those in her lifetime!

Though he'd desperately wanted to sweep her up into a tight embrace and kiss her speechless, he had successfully (though with great effort) fought back the urge. He dared not ruin any chance he might have to win her affections. After all, she had not earned the title of the "Unmatchable" Miss Mirabella for nothing. He told himself he'd best remember that.

He reached down to retrieve his sketch pad from the grass, decided not to waste time bothering about the charcoals, and turned to untether his mount from the latch of the swing gate.

A moment later, he joined Mirabella and her maid in the field. Annie was chattering nonstop, pointing to a distant line of trees where, she swore, she'd seen the tiger running.

Beyond the trees, Blackwood knew, lay a sprawling meadow where Penelope's sheep often grazed. The meadow marched with the grounds of Stormhaven. If they didn't soon find that tiger, he

The Unmatchable Miss Mirabella 153

thought, Penelope and her many guests might be witness to a nasty scene! He suggested they begin their search at once.

They looked for nearly an hour, but located nothing more than a few prints in the soft earth and several shredded tree branches.

"Are you certain it was Sasha you saw?" Mirabella asked Annie. "My tiger could have passed through here yesterday for all we know."

Annie nodded forcefully. "It was yer tiger, Miss Bella, I 'ave no doubt."

"Well, the animal is gone now," said Blackwood. He noted the frown on Mirabella's fair brow. "But never fear," he added quickly "I shall not rest until I find your tiger, Bella."

Now why had he gone and made such a promise? he wondered. If indeed he could even locate the beast, how did he possibly intend to *capture* it?

But a promise was a promise. And for Mirabella, he would do anything—even try and catch a tiger by its tail!

They returned to Stormhaven shortly before six, Annie muttering about being a day behind in her work, and Mirabella far too weary even to chastise her for carrying on so.

Of the trio, only Blackwood seemed undefeated by their lengthy walk and unsuccessful search. He also appeared preoccupied as he bade Mirabella good-bye near the front door.

Mirabella, thinking he wanted to be free of her presence, thanked him for his gallantry of the day and hastened inside, pulling Annie after her.

"Lawks, Miss Bella!" exclaimed Annie, "Did you 'ave t' be so quick t' leave 'is lordship's side? He was all for offerin' for you!"

Mirabella clicked her tongue and headed for the stairs. "Don't be silly, Annie. He was merely playing the gentleman. I am not so foolish as to believe anything else. All I want to do now is retire to my chamber and rest. I'd rather not think about Lord Blackwood or what transpired this afternoon."

"Yes, Miss Bella," said Annie, following Mirabella upstairs.

Within moments of undressing with Annie's help, Mirabella fell into a fitful sleep. She did not awaken until it was time to dress and go down for dinner. Annie appeared again to help her into a simple gown and brush Mirabella's hair until it shone with lustrous lights.

"Smile, Miss Bella," suggested Annie. "You always used t' tell me that a smile 'elps make any bad day a better one."

Mirabella indulged the maid, but found it hard to keep the smile affixed to her mouth as she descended to the dining room below and found Lord Blackwood conversing with Aunt Nellie.

Penelope looked up, beamed at the sight of her goddaughter, and moved to greet her. "I was hoping you'd feel rested enough to join us, my dear! Christian was just telling me of the awful ordeal young Robertshaw suffered this day. I must say, I was in a tither when he presented himself on my doorstep, swollen from ant bites! Not to worry, though. I immediately summoned the physician from Stow. He is even now overseeing Robertshaw's care. A few more poultices of bread and milk, and an hour or two of the spa waters, and young Robertshaw shall be right as rain, I predict!"

Mirabella cringed as she thought of Robertshaw being inundated with milk-soddened bread poultices. Poor dear. She would visit his sickroom in the morning, she promised herself.

Blackwood, however, was not of a mind to allow Mirabella to stew overly much where

The Unmatchable Miss Mirabella 155

Robertshaw was concerned. He executed a jaunty bow in her direction, and then was immediately at her side, guiding her to her seat along the polished table with its flaming candelabra and three settings.

"I thought we would dispense with entertaining the masses and just enjoy each other's company this night," said Penelope, taking her seat at the head of the table. "My other guests will be served a late supper in the East Wing, as I've arranged a very special evening for them. You don't mind just the three of us dining together, do you, Bella?"

Mirabella smiled. "Of course not, Aunt Nellie," she murmured. Silently, she prayed that the dinner would pass quickly and that she would be free of Blackwood's presence as soon as possible.

Much to her surprise, the meal proved to be pleasant and entertaining. Blackwood spoke easily of his travels in the Far East and even prompted Mirabella to share her own stories of her journey to that far-off place. She found herself sharing incidents from her trip that she'd half-forgotten until Blackwood had reminded her.

Much later, they adjourned to the front sitting room for a game of cards—with Mirabella winning every game of whist, and Blackwood sharing private smiles with her at her shrewdness—and then a smiling Penelope told them she'd had quite enough of losing card games to her goddaughter. Penelope excused herself, leaving the door ajar behind her and hinting that Mirabella and Christian should not tarry too long.

Blackwood caught Mirabella's eyes as Penelope departed. "There is nearly a full moon out tonight," he told her, getting to his feet and flinging open the windows. "Look," he said. "The sky is filled with sparkling stars."

Unable to help herself, Mirabella moved to

stand at the window beside him. She glanced up at the dark, twinkling canopy above Stormhaven.

"You see beauty in the night, don't you?" he asked.

She remembered when she had met him in the Gypsy's tent and they had talked of such things. Had it just been a mere day or so ago that they'd met? Amazing. It felt like a lifetime—time enough for her to realize that she'd come to know Blackwood, to understand him ... and perhaps even to fall in love with him.

"I believe I see beauty in every night," Mirabella murmured, afraid to give in to the warm soft feelings Blackwood's presence induced in her.

"What a gift," he whispered. "What a lovely way of viewing each night." He hesitated, then, clearly on a whim, he said, "Dance with me, Bella."

Her heart lurched. "But there's no music."

"We shall create our own music."

Mirabella's head swam, her heart hammered in her chest, and her blood surged through her veins. "This ... this is most unlike you. Your request is ... is most odd."

"Is it?"

She nodded. "When I first met you, you described the night sky as being scarred by broken stars."

"But that was then," he murmured, taking her by the hand, leading her from the sitting room to the terrace. "And this is ... ah, this is here and now."

He pulled her close, his arms fitting easily around her. "Dance with me, Bella," Blackwood urged, the scent of him, his heat, encompassing her.

She fell into the rhythm he created, felt her entire body—and even her soul—mesh with his.

And they danced, beneath the windows of Stormhaven, beneath the stars, and soon Mirabella could hear nothing but her own wildly beating heart strumming in her ears.

This was madness, she thought. It wouldn't do at all to appear more reckless than he already believed her to be.

Of a sudden, she pulled away. "I should go in now," she whispered.

"Yes," he agreed. His gaze was shuttered, hiding his innermost thoughts.

Mirabella felt burned to the quick by the sight of that unreadable gaze. She hastened away, fearing she'd made a total fool of herself in his eyes.

Blackwood watched her hasty exit, and all at once, his heart swelled with joy. He loved the Unmatchable Miss Mirabella, as surely as he breathed the air surrounding him!

Mirabella was obviously trying hard not to appear so reckless in his eyes, just as he was attempting not to be such a stuffy, top-lofty gentleman. And though the night had ended with her scurrying into the house, Blackwood knew that they'd proved themselves true: they were both trying to mesh their differences so that they could perhaps enjoy the best in each other.

His future was looking brighter by the moment. Whistling a happy tune, Blackwood set off into the night. If there was one way of making the Unmatchable Miss Mirabella realize the two of them were meant to be together, it was for him to find her tiger. He would take on the chivalric quest of delivering the beast to his beauty . . . and then—ah, then, he would tell her how much he loved her!

Mirabella again found herself in her room, wondering about Blackwood. What had made him change his arrogant ways? What force had prompted him suddenly to be playful and teasing? She was only thankful that she'd departed his company as quickly as she had; otherwise, she might have done something as foolish as to admit that she'd fallen in love with him!

Love? Imagine that, she marveled. After all the years of trying to avoid her many suitors, she'd actually fallen in love with a man whom she'd barely met and who had hardly pursued her!

She threw herself down on her bed and spent a long while staring at the canopy above her, seeing in her mind's eye Blackwood's smile, his enigmatic gaze, his handsome features.

Much later, she heard the strains of a not-so-distant violin. 'Twas a sound Mirabella knew only too well.

The Gypsy!

Mirabella slid off the bed and moved to the window. The Gypsy's song was too pretty to ignore. She pulled back the curtains and peered out into the moon-washed night.

The Gypsy stood under a tree immediately beneath her, scraping fervently away on the violin. His gaze was trained on her window and, at the first sight of her, he played an exultant crescendo, in celebration of her coming to listen to him at all.

He lowered his instrument with a deep bow. "Greetings!" he called up to her. " 'Tis I, Tomislav Karoly Jozsef Vilaghy! I have come to play you a Gypsy love song, my precious lady!"

Such contrived romanticism! Mirabella thought, but she smiled down at him nonetheless. She reminded him that he was, in fact, playing his tune upon a *stolen* violin, to which the Gypsy merely shrugged and gave a sheepish grin.

"You like my song, no?" he asked. "She comes

from the heart!" He clasped the instrument to his chest and then, quite suddenly, threw himself down on one knee. "I, Tomislav Karoly Jozsef Vilaghy—"

"Please," said Mirabella, wishing to forestall him, "let me just address you as Tommy, may I not? And pray, do not say again that you have fallen helplessly in love with me."

"But I, Tomislav Karoly Jozsef Vilaghy, have very much fallen in love with you, precious lady! I have spent my day thinking only of you ... of your lips ... of your shining hair!"

So much for shortening his name, she thought. And so much for dispensing with further proposals!

She was considering sending the Gypsy away, pleasant love songs and all, but his next words were too intriguing to ignore.

"I have brought you a gift, my precious lady!" he said. "You will be pleased! My gift, she is a spaniel just like the one you searched for at the fair!"

"A spaniel?" Mirabella said.

Grinning from ear to ear, he bent to retrieve a small box Mirabella hadn't noticed before. He flipped open the lid and scooped out a very familiar looking pup.

"I, Tomislav Karoly Jozsef Vilaghy, found the spaniel in this very garden! She is yours, is she not?"

Lord, I hope so, thought Mirabella. "Please," she called, "wait there. I am coming down."

The Gypsy was only too happy to oblige.

Mirabella whirled away from the window, and hastened to the gardens below.

The Gypsy, violin in one hand and the pup in the other, swept her another low bow as she rushed toward him.

"Ah, she is the gift you desired, no?" he asked, straightening.

"Yes, yes!" said Mirabella. She happily took the pup from his hold and gathered it close. "Oh, you naughty pup!" she whispered. "Have you no idea of the trouble you've caused? I've a mind to take you back to the fair!"

The spaniel, blissfully unaware of the scolding it was receiving, nuzzled Mirabella's neck with its warm, wet nose. It proved to be exactly the right thing to do. Mirabella felt her heart soften. She could no more return the pup to the fair than she could continue to scold it. Sighing, she pressed a kiss to its head and lovingly scratched one of its silky ears.

"I have pleased you!" exclaimed the Gypsy. "I see the gladness in your eyes. Your heart, does it not now beat with love for me? I can bring you another spaniel. I will! I, Tomislav Karoly Jozsef Vilaghy, shall bring you a *dozen* spaniels!"

"No!" Mirabella said, alarmed. "That won't be necessary. Trust me when I tell you that one is more than enough."

"I have won your heart with but one spaniel? Ah, our courtship, she is now complete!" He placed the violin on the ground, then plucked the pup from Mirabella's arms and replaced it in the box. "I kiss you now and then we marry, eh?" Before Mirabella could react, the Gypsy swept her into his arms and crushed her to his chest.

13

Blackwood limped down the winding path that led to Penelope's gardens. His left thigh felt on fire. His once-natty attire was dirt-stained and sported tears here and there; his formerly creaseless neckcloth was now so much wrinkled linen. In spite of all this, his lordship was actually smiling. Beaming in fact. The reason for his high spirits trailed happily alongside him, with a leather leash looped about the ruff of its neck, and was purring softly.

"Come along, Sasha," said Blackwood. "I know of a certain beauty who will be overjoyed to see you."

Not missing a beat, the tiger softly bumped its large head against his lordship's leg. Blackwood rewarded the beast with a generous scratch between the shoulder blades.

They'd become fast friends. How could they not? thought his lordship, pleased. One did not climb stone walls and crawl under hedgerows after a tiger without coming to know the animal!

After seeing Mirabella safely to bed, Blackwood had spent an hour or more searching for the tiger. He'd determined that finding the errant Sasha was one mission he would accomplish with both swiftness and ease. Of course, the swiftness with which he'd located the tiger was debatable. As for the ease of the mission ... well, that was *thoroughly* debatable. 'Twas a bloody difficult thing, capturing tigers!

All in all, though, Blackwood concluded that his night had gone well enough. Sasha was now proving to be obedient and lovable (after she'd chewed the end of another of his rosewood canes, though Blackwood wasn't complaining, for it had been the cane that had finally enticed the tiger his way). Blackwood was looking forward to the moment when he could present Mirabella with her pet.

Suddenly, he heard her cry out. The sound came from somewhere within Penelope's gardens.

Fearing for her safety, Blackwood broke into a run, Sasha sprinting alongside him. He charged into the gardens, saw Mirabella being manhandled by the Gypsy, and spoke without thinking.

"If you value your life," he cried, "you will unhand the lady this instant!"

Mirabella, who only a moment ago had feared for her virtue, rejoiced at the sound of Blackwood's voice. She turned around, wanting to see his face, to prove he had truly come to her rescue and she wasn't just imagining things. But the Gypsy, though he'd released her from his tight embrace, took her hands in his and forced her attention back toward him.

"A thousand pardons, my precious lady!" he said. "Forgive me. I meant you no harm. I had thought you loved me ... but now I can see you do not. I see only the passion you have for your lover, and he for you! I go now. I leave you to each other."

He released Mirabella's hands, and stooped to retrieve the violin from the ground. With a nervous gaze, he peered round her skirt toward Blackwood. "I go now, see? No harm done. And the duel we speak of earlier? We forget it, eh? Your lady, she is fine! She is in love with you and you with her. You be together. You be happy!"

"Not so fast!" said Blackwood.

Mirabella, alarmed by the tone of his lordship's voice, spun to face him. The sight she beheld nearly took her breath away.

He stood before her, his hair windblown, his neckcloth askew, and his once-polished Hessians spotted with mud. He held a leather leash in one fist ... and at the other end of that leash stood a very complacent Sasha.

"Christian! You have found my tiger!"

He nodded, but he was obviously not thinking about the tiger at the moment. He looked to the Gypsy, who still hid behind Mirabella's skirts.

A dangerous light lit his dark eyes. "Come out from behind there, man," he said. "I would like a word with you. Alone."

"Christian, no!" said Mirabella. His lordship looked angry enough to resort to fisticuffs with the Gypsy. "Please, do not be upset. I'm fine, truly I am. He didn't hurt me. Let us just forget the incident."

Suddenly the Gypsy rose to his feet. "You listen to your lady, yes? She speaks the truth! I go now. I, Tomislav Karoly Jozsef Vilaghy, will trouble you no more!"

"See that you don't," said Blackwood. Though he clearly thought better of the notion, his lordship motioned for the Gypsy to leave.

But the Gypsy could not resist a final bow in Mirabella's direction.

Unfortunately, his movements—and the instrument he held in one hand—caught Sasha's eye. The tiger took one look at the violin bow and, perhaps thinking it was yet another rosewood cane, gave a mighty leap toward the thing.

"*Aiyeee!*" cried the Gypsy. He made a beeline for

the nearest tree, grabbed the lowest branch, and swung up into the leafy bower. He squatted, cowering, against the trunk of the tree.

Blackwood smiled. He'd had a tight hold to Sasha's leash all the while. Thoroughly enjoying himself, he unrolled a length of the leather, giving Sasha enough lead to stand on her hind paws against the tree trunk and to playfully bat at the Gypsy's feet.

"Christian," scolded Mirabella, "the man is frightened half to death!"

"As he deserves to be, for frightening you," said Blackwood.

"I am fine, Christian. I told you that."

"Then damn the man for frightening *me*," he said. The knuckles of his fists turned white as he gripped the leash.

"Christian, w-what's come over you?"

"I didn't like finding you in his arms, Bella. I didn't like it at all. And when I thought of him perhaps kissing you, touching you as I never have, I liked it even less."

He raked his free hand through his hair, blew out a sigh, and was unable to hold back his feelings any longer.

"I have a confession to make," he said, his voice suddenly rich with emotion. "You see, my dear, dear Bella, I have gone and done something many others before me have done ... I've fallen in love with you. Indeed, I find I love you more with each passing moment. I want to share sunlight with you, and starlight and moonlight. I want yours to be the first face I see in the morning and the last I see at night. I want you for my love, and for my life. Bella, my dear, sweet, Bella, will you do me the honor of becoming my wife?"

Tears of joy filled her eyes and a quaver of heartfelt emotion roughened her voice. "Yes, yes, a thousand times yes!" she whispered, and though the words were a cliché, they were heartfelt.

Suddenly, she was smiling and crying all at once. "Oh, Christian, after the moment in the meadow when you didn't kiss me, I thought that perhaps you wanted nothing more to do with me."

"Ah, Bella, never, ever that." He moved close, his hands slipping up her arms, Sasha's leash trailing. "I wanted to kiss you—have wanted to kiss you again ever since I first did so in that blasted tent."

"So why didn't you?"

"At first, because I was a fool, but later 'twas because I did not wish to frighten the Unmatchable Miss Mirabella away."

"I am not so unmatchable, my lord."

"I know that now," he said, smiling. He slid his hands up the long, slender column of her throat, his fingers lacing behind her neck. "I love you, Bella. With all my heart and soul, I love you."

"And I love you."

He rested his forehead against hers, then allowed himself a moment of pure pleasure in just gazing into her beautiful blue eyes.

"Christian?"

"Hmmm?"

"If you don't kiss me soon, I swear I shall die from longing!"

Blackwood's mobile mouth curved into a grin. And then, his thumbs caressing her jaw, he lowered his lips to hers. 'Twas a soft kiss at first, feathery-light and meant to entice. But the taste of her, the sweetness, caused him to deepen the contact. Dropping Sasha's leash, he allowed his arms to circle protectively around her. Mirabella melted against him, returning his kiss, and soon they were lost to passion.

Sasha, meanwhile, felt the slack in her leash and happily started to climb the tree. The Gypsy gave a yelp of despair.

Penelope Barrington stepped into the gardens at that very moment to see what all the fuss was about.

"Bella?" she called. "Is that you making this ruckus?"

Penelope had just concluded a thrillingly successful séance in the east wing. She wore a comely gown of crimson that did little to conceal her generous curves. In her hands she carried a large crystal ball (for effect only, of course, since no true spirit was ever beckoned via a sphere of crystal, she knew!) and atop her blonde hair sat a black turban which sported a huge uncut ruby. As always, she held a pipe clamped tight betwixt her pearly-white teeth, and the scent of clove tobacco wafted about her.

Mirabella, hearing her godmama's voice, momentarily pulled her mouth away from Blackwood's.

"Hullo, Auntie," she said.

Penelope, taking one look at her goddaughter in the earl's embrace, and espying not only the tiger but also the lost pup and the Gypsy as well, grinned.

"Having an adventure, Bella?" she asked.

"I believe, Auntie, that my adventures have only just begun. Christian brought Sasha home . . . and he has asked me to marry him."

"To which you replied in the affirmative, I take it."

"Yes," whispered Mirabella, smiling up at Blackwood.

Penelope gave a wink in Blackwood's direction. "So you managed to capture both her tiger *and* her heart in one fell swoop, did you? Famous! I knew you could. Welcome to the family, my dear boy—though, you know, you always have been family to me."

"Thank you, Nellie," said Blackwood, still holding tight to Mirabella. He motioned toward the crystal ball in her hands. "Do not say that you have been contacting spirits tonight."

"Perish the thought! *They* contact *me*. The crystal seems to fascinate my guests, so I always keep one near at hand. I've several others in my study ... I say," she added, noticing a pair of handsome masculine legs dangling from beneath the tree's branches, "might that gentleman have need of assistance?"

"Oh!" said Mirabella. "I had quite forgotten about him. Christian, do you not think the man has suffered enough? You should not have let go of Sasha's leash!"

Blackwood caressed Mirabella's cheek. "But you were so adamant about finally being kissed that I—"

"Christian," she warned.

"Oh, very well."

To Mirabella's surprise, he did not hasten after the trailing end of the tiger's leash. Instead, he merely called out the beast's name.

Sasha, hearing her new master's gentle call, slid down the trunk of the tree and dutifully loped over to plop herself down at Blackwood's feet.

Mirabella shook her head in wonder. "Who would have ever imagined? The two of you make quite a pair."

"We do at that," he agreed. "But," he added, holding her close once again, "I do believe you and I make an even better match!"

So saying, he commenced to kiss her again.

A pleased Penelope left the lovebirds to themselves and wandered over to stand beneath the tree.

The Gypsy took one look at her and forgot all about the dangerous tiger. He jumped to the ground, clasped the violin to his breast, and threw himself down on bended knee before her.

"Allow me to introduce myself, precious lady. Tomislav Karoly Jozsef Vilaghy! I am in love with you! Prepare to fall equally in love with me!"

Penelope gazed at the Gypsy with a woman's appreciation of his handsome good looks.

"I don't suppose you know any love songs?" she said.

He beamed. "Ah ... yes!" And he began to scrape away at the violin, playing a fervent melody.

Penelope was a captivated audience.

Blackwood, holding Mirabella's lithe form in his strong embrace, could not help but laugh.

"So that is all a gentleman need do to win a lady's attention, is it?" he asked. He considered a moment and then, his eyes glowing with passion, pulled her ever closer, whispering huskily, " 'Tis I, Christian Phillip Edward White, Earl of Blackwood. I am in love with you ... prepare to fall equally in love with me, my precious lady!"

Mirabella teasingly avoided his kiss. "Ah, my lord, I fear you are too late. You see, I have already fallen in love."

"Oh?"

"Yes," said Mirabella. She lifted one hand to lovingly caress his cheek. "I fear I have fallen in love with a certain gentleman I met at the fair in Stow. Though he did prove woefully inept at tangling with a dancing bear, he proved far more adept at capturing my heart."

Blackwood grinned. "How I adore you, Bella."

"And I you, my love."

With a low growl of pleasure, Blackwood tightened his hold and then, with a deep and mind-numbing kiss, he began to show is once-Unmatchable Miss Mirabella just how very much he adored her.

Neither of them noticed when the pup, ever playful, scooted out of its box and dashed after the trailing end of the leash Sasha was contentedly chomping upon. The mischievous pup took up the leash and gave it a tug. Sasha sat up and purred. The pup wagged its tail. And then the two dashed happily off into the night.

Avon Regency Romance

Kasey Michaels

THE CHAOTIC MISS CRISPINO
76300-1/$3.99 US/$4.99 Can

THE DUBIOUS MISS DALRYMPLE
89908-6/$2.95 US/$3.50 Can

THE HAUNTED MISS HAMPSHIRE
76301-X/$3.99 US/$4.99 Can

Loretta Chase

THE ENGLISH WITCH 70660-1/$2.95 US/$3.50 Can
ISABELLA 70597-4/$2.95 US/$3.95 Can
KNAVES' WAGER 71363-2/$3.95 US/$4.95 Can
THE SANDALWOOD PRINCESS
71455-8/$3.99 US/$4.99 Can

THE VISCOUNT VAGABOND
70836-1/$2.95 US/$3.50 Can

Jo Beverley

EMILY AND THE DARK ANGEL
71555-4/$3.99 US/$4.99 Can

THE FORTUNE HUNTER
71771-9/$3.99 US/$4.99 Can

THE STANFORTH SECRETS
71438-8/$3.99 US/$4.99 Can

Buy these books at your local bookstore or use this coupon for ordering:

Mail to: Avon Books, Dept BP, Box 767, Rte 2, Dresden, TN 38225   C
Please send me the book(s) I have checked above.
❏ My check or money order— no cash or CODs please— for $_____is enclosed
(please add $1.50 to cover postage and handling for each book ordered— Canadian residents add 7% GST).
❏ Charge my VISA/MC Acct#_____Exp Date_____
Minimum credit card order is two books or $6.00 (please add postage and handling charge of $1.50 per book — Canadian residents add 7% GST). For faster service, call 1-800-762-0779. Residents of Tennessee, please call 1-800-633-1607. Prices and numbers are subject to change without notice. Please allow six to eight weeks for delivery.

Name_____
Address_____
City_____State/Zip_____
Telephone No._____

REG 0693